Jay Horne's

THE

DEATH OF SCIENCE

A Novel Introduction to Rootworld

A Novel of Rootworld

PRESENTED BY BOOKFLURRY INC.

The Death of Science: A Novel Introduction to Rootworld

Martha D. Horne, Cover Artist

Cataloguing Publication Data

Horne, Jay M., 1980-

> *The Death of Science / Jay M. Horne*

ISBN: 978-0-9963227-7-5

Library of Congress Control Number: 2023905225

Bookflurry Inc. Publishing does not participate in, endorse, or have any authority or responsibility concerning private business affairs between the author and the public.

> *All mail addressed to the author will be forwarded but the publisher cannot, unless specifically instructed by the author, give out an address or phone number.*

Bookflurry Inc.

Bradenton, FL

This book is dedicated to three Greats,
Terry Pratchett (may he rest in peace among other
Knights),
Piers Anthony, and Stephen King.

Also, four other Greats,
Montanna, Ashton, Morgan, and Jaymat.

Prologue

The year was exactly 0000 A.D. when everything went to hell.

You'd have to be Jewish or Druish to enjoy that statement, but let's continue to consider that the audience is normal. Not that Jews and Drews aren't normal. They just wear weird shoes and different kinds of hats.

By normal, let's say generally American and not entirely in the know when it comes to biblical fact. And if you were born on any other continent, then you will already know that this book is going to be upside down from the get-go.

Okay. The Britons might think this all sounds rather realistic, but they will only be fans because they are just as ignorant as us Americans. If man evolved from monkeys, I think we've evolved from Brits. Don't be angry, just say cheers, because we all know that the true measure of intelligence is not how much you can remember, but rather, how much you can remember while imbibing on as many dissociatives, inebriants, or pan galactic gargle blasters as possible.

It all started when Hazeus refused to drink wine at the last supper. That rubbed everyone quite wrong. To be fair though, he was only trying to make a statement that went right over the heads of everyone present. And by present, I mean presently drunk.

He also refused his last meal. Which was a thing unheard of! Even today, the worst of criminals get their last meal just the way they like it. It's considered humane.

But Hazeus was trying to make a point. Bodily desires keep one apart from their Roots. And in everyone's roots there exists a vein of magic.

How terrible it must have been to see the son of God, who'd become flesh, being hoisted up on a cross and subjected to suffering after such a terribly uncomfortable truth being portrayed.

Alas, there was wine there to ease the pain for his disciples though they would quickly begin to wonder just how it was that they used to turn water into it by a simple wave of the hand.

That is because, with the death of Hazeus came another death. The death of magic.

Not many years after Hazeus emerged from his tomb, he would get word that the Roman Catholic Church had begun celebrating his resurrection with a tradition called Holy Communion; an act in which believers partake of wine and bread right at the altar in his holy name!

It was then that the son of God returned home to Mom and Dad and the people of misguided planet Earth falsely witnessed our Lord ascending into Heaven, as it was they, who actually descended...

Okay, okay, we won't go that far!

Earth did not go to hell, per say. God just did the only thing he could to the people of Earth. Hazeus's parents did what any good parents would do with a child's early playthings. They put them in storage.

In a place that mankind could cool down while Hazeus grew up a bit and could better understood the reality of things. A reality that all beings must eventually face.

That certain reality that we put off as long as we can. The reality that we are ourselves ultimately responsible for what happens in our own universes.

There are many epic tales of Rootworld, but the first that is important to understand is one of a man and woman in the late twentieth century who stumbled upon two magic relics that wielded the power of raising the ancient tower of Babel.

The late twentieth century and early twenty first century were a trying time for humanity. They were approaching the point of blooming scientific discovery. A time when the entropy of the universe had become so compounded that science could no longer keep up with explaining things to everyone. Even with a world-wide-web, disinformation was preventing humanity from agreeing on any one belief system.

Some still believed that aliens would invade. Some believed that no God existed at all. Some believed that you could drive three husbands to divorce in hopes that they would pay your bills and going to church on Sundays would wash you clean of sin. Some divorced husbands believed that pan galactic gargle blasters solved all the problems in the universe!

It was an age that Father Time and Mother Earth had been waiting on for a long time. An event that meant their baby boy, Hazeus, was ready to be sent off to college!

It was during this time that something magical happened. And nothing magical had happened on Earth for thousands of years!

Young Jesse and Evelyn, drawn together in Love from different races and continents, succeeded in returning the relics to their origin and the Great Pyramid of Giza twisted up from under the Earth, revealing its true massive form as the tower of Babel that touched the sky.

In this moment, the continents of the great planet Earth were re-converged into one supercontinent, Pangea, and in surviving cities it was declared, firstly by a newly sober Pope, that Science was indeed Magic.

Introduction

Forty years after the Convergence, a girl named Kristen leaned left and crossed over a crumbled part of sidewalk bearing the painted remains of a permanent hopscotch course. The dark clouds had abated and were replaced with the shifting pink and blue of the barrier. Her yellow rain slicker flapped along the bottom edges as she pedaled her rusted bicycle through the intersection of twelfth and twelfth in what was still known as Bradenton, Florida.

On her back, wedged between her shoulders and her school bag, was a paintball gun loaded with enough ammo to bring down the house. She'd do battle with the boys at three o'clock behind the elementary side of the school, but she had played hooky this morning in order to go jump off the bridge with two of her other friends; they'd stood her up.

Ditching solo was the pits, but she'd already called in as her mother so was stuck riding things out till closing bell this afternoon. She was just going to have to try her best to stay busy and not think about her father. He probably would have let her ditch if it would have made her feel better.

The Village of the Arts used to be a happening place thirty years ago. History said there was a circus, a gem mine, and a mildly successful rejuvenation attempt of the area back in two thousand twenty, but now it was as vacant as a graveyard here. After the great flood, nothing really put back down roots in the area.

But the buildings were all still there. Even the old multi-directional sign, with its parrot on top, stood like a fossil. Petrified there like some old dinosaur bone sticking up from the tar pits.

She passed by the sign, which was now unreadable, and saw what she was looking for up on the hill. It was an old well behind what used to be Nan's curiosities. The decorative roof long gone. The top sealed with thick iron doors and a chain.

Nan's curiosities used to be town center to the Village of the Arts. Now, it was just, well, center, minus the town, and everyone knew to stay away from it. What was left of it existed beneath the all-encompassing roots of a giant banyan tree, which she pedaled cautiously up toward.

The real reason you stayed away was because of the squatters. According to her mother, there were probably meth heads, and child molesters living in it now.

There wasn't an honest job in the area for miles, besides at the K-12 learning facility, and the only safe place to live was directly across from it in the campus condominiums. Education was the only blue-collar job inside of the barrier, if you counted out carpentry, hospitality, and a handful of social services. Private sector stuff was pretty much nil unless you crossed the Memorial Skybridge, and for that you needed a visa.

At least she didn't see any perverts yet. Just a bunch of dirt and roots. And the road was mostly torn to hell. Not that anyone used these roads anymore. The school watchman had a motorized six-wheeler but you could see it coming from a mile away with its one ultra bright headlamp that could literally light something on fire if turned to its high-beam. As of yet, the sun hadn't gotten too high so the humidity was keeping the sand from kicking up into plumes like it ordinarily would.

There weren't any curbs since the Continental Convergence caused the flood, as no clean-up effort had made it this far out, so all of the mud that settled along the gutters and against the structures had just been left there to weather itself away over the years. By noon, things would be drier and get a lot more dusty, even though it was still cool.

It used to be considered a beach town. The gulf had been only ten or so miles to the east, evidenced by the sediment, made up of a lot of crumbled seashells.

She dropped her bike, pretty confident that the rumors her parents had told her had been bull crap.

Who'd squat out here? What would you survive on?

She passed by a few sickly-looking palmettos as she strode up to the giant legs of the banyan. After ducking under the strange tendrils hanging from above and into the shade of the underbelly of the great behemoth, she could see the brick making up the backside of the forgotten shop of curiosities. It had been tagged with spray paint. What could be seen of the wall was now a giant skull with its mouth open, reminding her of a print she'd once seen of the Grateful dead.

Pretty impressive, she thought, then wondered if the graffiti had been intentional or vandalism. It did have a freshness that didn't jive well with the rest of the hideout though. Well, she couldn't have suspected that she'd be the only one to ever play hooky back here, could she? She poked her head back out from the tree's hanging vines and looked around again. Then decided this would do.

She ran down and grabbed her bike and lifted it up over the small rise from the road onto the abandoned backlot, then made her way back to the hiding place. Spread the vines and pushed her bike inside. Then she took off her bag and slung it down by the brick wall, parked her bike in front of the huge skull mural and took off her slicker. It was a little warmer in here.

She decided to fold up the raincoat and use it as a cushion to sit on while she did a little art of her own.

She placed her cushion next to her bag so she could lean against the wall and pulled her backpack into her lap, being mindful of the paintball gun. Yeah, she could have a hell of a time shooting up this place, but that's not the kind of girl Kristen was. She liked art, illegal or no. Besides, she was set on spending at least half of her ammunition on John, who had shot her directly in the nipple last weekend.

Instead, she put the semi-automatic air rifle down beside her and rummaged through her sack to find her creative writing journal.

"Where in the hell?" she said, digging. Then she paused, thinking she heard something.

Was that laughter? Was someone laughing at her irritation?

She thought better of it and continued on. She pushed aside her Magic is Science textbook, her folder where her assignments are marked daily, which she was planning on forging sometime this morning, her facemask for paintball, her pencil box, her cell phone. She pushed it all back to the other side and heard the jingle of the co2 cartridges at the bottom of the bag. She reached all the way to the bottom— and then paused.

There it was again. Someone *was* laughing.

"Damn it!" she said and dumped the bag out on the ground along the wall.

The stationary piled out of the bag onto the packed shelly sand and the aluminum co2 canisters jingled down after them, careening off one another.

She gave the bag one last irritable shake and a final cartridge came down hard, striking the butt of her gun. She went rigid when the cartridge ruptured.

For a split second she thought she might have been bitten by a snake! Sand had blasted her all over and a loud sharp puffing sound filled her ears with cotton and then sent them ringing. She hardly had time to yelp before she realized what had happened. Instinctively, she began knuckling her eye sockets before a gentle laughter started up from inside of her.

The cartridge had shot clear out of the tree fort!

Then she was blinking the sand free from her eyelids, and when she realized she was okay she started laughing and dusting off her textbook and other little things. My god, it wasn't a snake, she thought as the ringing subsided. And Jesus, what if it had been the gun going off? She coulda shot her own eye out like that kid in the old Christmas show! She stood up under the banyan's embrace and dusted off her shorts and shirt. Then pulled out her ponytail holder and shook out her wavy red hair.

Little did she know that she wasn't the first carrot top to sit right here and see what she was about to discover.

While Kristen was pulling her hair back into a pony, she was looking at the spot in the sediment that the cartridge had blasted against the wall, inevitably sending itself flying free. There was a horseshoe shape of dirt missing against the base of the brick, and instead of more brick, there was something else there.

Kristen knelt and pushed away the sand on either side of the void with her palms. She put her face down by her red sneaker and looked at her own reflection. It was a dingy reflection, but it was definitely a reflection.

She went to work digging away what she could and before too long she had an entire arc of plate glass and its rotting wooden trim exposed. A window!

She tried rubbing the mildew off of the glass with her fist. No good. She looked around for something to wipe it clean with. She wasn't ruining her shirt. Then she cupped her hands against the filthy glass and tried her best to make anything out but could see nothing. Then she did something that she wouldn't have done, had it been a few minutes ago and had her writing journal been in her bag. She actually surprised herself when she did it. And she did it without thinking.

She rolled over on her bottom and kicked the glass with the heels of her tennies.

The sound startled her. It was like breaking ice cubes from the tray in the freezer, and it felt naughty, as if her mother might come home and find that she'd broken the bathroom mirror or something. Then the glass hit the ground inside of the old building and a spray of twinkling noises came up to her from the hollow, making her imagine the pieces shatter into sand below.

A cool air enveloped her calves then danced up the front of her legs as she drew them back to turn on her knees and peer through. Her t-shirt billowed as she braced herself on the brick above and beside the window considering ducking her head inside.

She breathed out and then in. It was the smell you'd expect from an attic not a basement, but she supposed it was Florida, after all. Then, after a moment's consideration she got up and went and parted the vines, letting some of the light flood in from the east.

After tying them back to leave a split in the dry tendrils, she crossed back over to the opening, watching her shadow shorten against the wall into nothing as she knelt back down and peered inside.

Now she could see the spacious interior illuminated by an antique orange light, giving her the unique experience an archeologist may feel while glimpsing the inside of an ancient Egyptian pyramid for the first time in centuries.

There were piles of dusty, yet organized junk all around the room.

The back wall and floor were fashioned of sandstone with yellow and red inlaid tiles, all of it ancient. But there was something stark and clean that stood out from all of the other things down there. It was standing in the center of the room, a six-foot pile of tarnished rubbish behind it, a chest-high table at its side, and it was looking back at her from under a hooded cloak of pitch.

A Meeting with Death

Just behind a silver hood ornament shaped like the Grim reaper in flight, Death could see the rest of the late Nan's cache in the basement of her shop of curiosities. He could also see Kristen peering in from above. She might think he was hiding from her. But that would be as much rubbish as was piled up down here around him. Death doesn't hide. He does his work right out in the open, and with pride.

He only appears where and when he has a job to do.

He steps out from behind the pile of tarnished antiques and takes the hood ornament in his bony fingers as if to prove his point.

He looks toward the girl briefly, turning the small semblance of himself in his right hand while holding his scythe expertly in the palm of his left. He uses it like a walking stick, though he'd walk perfectly fine without it.

Not this one's time yet, he thinks, as he watches her get up and walk away from the broken window.

He takes a few paces to the center of the room and then the sunlight peeks through into his temporary dungeon up at ground level. Half of the panes of that window are covered in dirt as if the land was fashioned around this old building rather than the other way around.

If this were a real dungeon, there would only be one way in and out. But there happened to be one and a half. Behind the robed figure is the first. A doorway covered with a failing curtain of beads that once completed a gradient of Mexican design but now had a few bare strings that left dark slits in the pattern. The little plastic spheres had liberated themselves and now collected in corners and low parts of the architecture instead.

The other way in was a one-way portal at the back of a cave, but only the Grim Reaper could see that from his point of view and there was no need to bother the girl, who had now returned to the little window for a better look, with such things yet. He only knew it existed because he had come here by the same means as the rest of the dead and forgotten artifacts in this place.

He watched Kristen get down on to her belly and peer through the portal at him.

No. It wasn't her time, yet. But, he was here to kill *something*.

Kristen's hand went to the trigger of her air rifle.

"It won't do you any good, you know?" said the thing from down below her.

She was struck with horror and wonder simultaneously. Both feelings she had briefly became acquainted with this very summer, along with a little bit of love, maybe. She had never fled from those feelings before, and she wouldn't be starting now.

"It will just make a mess. Besides you are in no immediate danger up there," came the voice as if from the throat of some stone trombone.

"Why does your voice sound like you're in a cave?" Kristen asked.

The hooded figure moved its head slowly back and forth, surveying the cathedral-like space. That oddly made Kristen feel like she may be asking a stupid question.

"I get that all the time," it said. "But, to be fair, in this case I *am* standing in front of a cave so it may just be the acoustics." He was turning to look up at her.

Kristen could now see the bony outcrop of the thing's chin. "It's all echoey. And your…" Where his eyes should have been, there were two dark pits with only a tiny glimmer, much like a coin flipping at a varying rate of speed.

"Well, I once heard one of the other incarnations say that my voice echoes because it goes directly into your head," Death told her.

She thought about this when she realized his jaw bones hadn't been moving when he spoke.

Death turned his attention to the tall round wooden table. Then he gingerly placed the hood ornament that resembled himself down on to it. Also on the table are two other items. A statue of a raven and an old shoe, missing the toes. Death steadied the raven with one bleached finger after it rocked slightly, then he moved his sickle into his right hand.

"Since you are asking me, I think they can only be the result of one or two things." He said plainly.

"I'm not sure I follow you," said Kristen, now placing both hands up near the window hoping to show that she wasn't afraid, and also that she wasn't going to blast him with paintballs.

"The echoes, I mean," he began "they are either because, when the time comes to die, there is nothing left in your skull but the sound of my voice…"

All of a sudden, Death's stare was making her feel a lot more nervous. She was just starting to be more thankful that he was down there and she was up here when something strange crossed his countenance. A lipless smile. Just a parting of the jaw in such a way that it suggests that he is humored, really. But it was there for a moment.

Then he shrugged with his sickle arm and waved the tool absently in a gesture that precluded what came next.

"Or," says he, "there simply weren't that many brains there to—"

Death covers his mouth with his left hand for a moment and Kristen thinks he might vomit, then he lurches back and belts out,

"Or there simply weren't that many brains there to begin with!"

A great hollow breath of gusto comes from the skeletal figure and then it catches in his throat again,

"I do say! A hollow head makes for great acoustics!"

Kristen watched as Death placed his left hand on the wooden table to balance himself as he doubled over with laughter. The three items on the table began to shimmy and shake under his trembling hand.

The hood ornament rocked back and forth on its wings; its sickle held up before it like a flag of war. The Raven, crafted of some black onyx or obsidian teetered back and forth, threatening to tumble. The old shoelaces quivered. Then he finally caught his breath.

"Come now," Death remarked composing himself. "Aren't you the least bit curious?"

Just then Kristen had looked away from the odd sight and back out to where her stationary was piled in the dirt. She had turned her head in disbelief at the odd Grim Reaper's humor, and though she tried to muster a laugh, she was just too flabbergasted to do so. But when she had turned her head, she saw her cellphone lying there and grabbed it up quickly.

"Curious about what?" She said over her shoulder, turning only briefly to show she was interested in what this skeleton had to say.

"It won't work, you know?" came the hollow reverberating voice of Death again.

She was pressing her thumb down on the fingerprint scanner to unlock it and was proud to prove the skeleton wrong when she slid up the camera icon and turned it quickly toward the thing down there.

"Smile," she said tactfully and tapped the shutter icon on the screen.

There was a brief flash inside of the old shop of curiosities' storeroom. Death had merely held up a skeletal hand in front of his eyes. He wasn't wearing his shades.

"Uhg," Death sighed, lowering his hand as Kristen turned the phone and clicked the picture of the last photo to enlarge it.

There was nothing but a storeroom of junk!

"I tried telling you. It only works with Polaroid cameras," he said downtrodden. His tone of voice made her think of Eeyore from the Winnie the pooh cartoons they showed last year in the library. Then she saw something else lying there among the scattered contents of her schoolbag. Her creative writing notebook!

She plopped her cell down on top of her deflated backpack and grabbed the notebook. Then, with her other hand she searched through the pile for a writing utensil and knew she came upon it when her fingers brushed across the fuzzy end of her bunny rabbit ink pen. She looked back into the hole while pulling the cap of her ink pen off with her teeth and still couldn't possibly believe that the Death thing was still in there!

"That will do nicely," said the Death thing, tapping each of the items on the table with the tip of a bony appendage.

"Where should we start?" he asked, glancing back up at Kristen, who was clutching her notebook and pen, wishing she didn't have to lie here in the dirt on her belly to record this stuff. No one was going to believe her.

His ivory fingertip was resting on the statue of the raven.

"I think we should leave this one for the *future*," Death said, making Kristen feel like he knew something he wasn't telling her.

Of course, he knew things he wasn't telling her! Perhaps she could ask him when she was going to bite the big one? No. It was obvious that he would know those answers, but the way he said *future*, made her get the shivers all over.

"I think a premature Death may be a bit steep of a punishment for skipping school, Kristen," said Death.

"However, since we both happen to be here and we have plenty of time, we might as well kill something."

Kristen watched as the wraith propped his sickle against a pile of dusty wooden carvings. Some were birdhouses, perhaps, others were rocking horses or puppets. The scythe blended right in with the tangle of junk. Then he lifted the hood ornament into his hands.

"Allow me to be your substitute for the day."

He held the hood ornament up so she could get a good look at it in the light. A perfectly tiny silver replica of Death thrusting his sickle out with his robes flying behind. All that seemed to be missing was the car it belonged to.

"I trust you will take notes," he said and looked to see if she were prepared to jot into her creative writing journal. She was.

Death wasn't usually about killing other incarnations, but he supposed that they couldn't really destroy each other, not permanently anyway. However, there was that poor chap that he had killed to get his own position...

Whatever, let Fate hash that one out.

"Let us begin, then," Death announced.

"Wait!" Kristen said, holding her ink pen up.

She really was quite an attractive young girl. If he were only a few hundred years younger, he thought.

"What is it, now?"

"I thought you said we were going to kill something."

Ah! And ambitious at that! To be a few hundred years younger.

He dropped his hands a bit and held her gaze.

"Time, my young darling," he said, "We are here to kill, Time."

Then he started.

"Today's first lesson," he said, "has to do with the many pitfalls of taking boredom for granted..." and then the little silver coins in his eyes grew brighter and Kristen kinda felt like a deer in the headlights.

She could almost see white lines dashing by on a dark highway.

"I call this one Carpool," said Death. "You could say that I wrote it myself."

Then the echoes in his voice faded away and he sounded almost young again. When Kristen closed her eyes, she was certain she could see it.

CARPOOL
Chapter One

It was the umpteenth time that Mike and Steve had taken the turnpike seventy miles Northeast to their trailer out in Mount Juliet.

The highway was always the same. Grey slate, stretching out in the high beams. White lines dashing beneath the fenders of the old El Camino.

I-40 was always pretty lonely out on the eastbound side of Music City. The two boys were settled down into the impressions of old Chamille's bench. Mike, his arm stretched out along the leather seat back and one hand on the wheel. Steve snuggled into the crook between the passenger door and the seat belt hangar, his work jacket balled up so he could lay his head on it and just stare out the window.

He'd watch the lines in the road slide by, sometimes skating to and fro, for no better reason than Mike getting bored with one lane or another. Dodging invisible traffic.

They both listened to the deceitful silence of the road. Full of repetitive noises that had become background sound. The rumble of the v-8. The whine of rubber on the asphalt like a faraway airplane propeller. And Dave Matthews, barely playing in the speakers.

Seventy miles wasn't a terrible work commute. An hour and a half maybe, though they had been known to make it in fifty minutes, racing in separate cars.

Those times, they were lucky to have made it alive, between the weather and the deer.

Eventually, they had decided it was safer to carpool.

You could motor out another ten hours down I-40 and eventually it'd dump you out in the Atlantic Ocean near Wilmington, North Carolina. Not too far from the Bermuda triangle.

On the night of the last full moon before Halloween, the Ley Line that runs along the I-40 highway is especially active.

On this night, half an hour into their monotonous drive home, both boys were feeling a little like they were driving straight through the Bermuda Triangle, now.

A school bus passed, headed westbound.

"Holy shit," Mike said, "did ya see that?"

It had been painted white and the windows were tinted dark like Chamille's, except the bus's tint was torn all along the windows facing this side.

"That was creepy man," Mike said.

Steve craned his neck up like a cat shocked from a nap. "What? That bus?"

"Yeah, man," said Mike, "looked like there were a bunch of people pressed up against the windows in there."

He had been looking back over his left shoulder and then into the side view, watching the red lights disappear over the horizon.

"What's a school bus doing out this late anyhow?" asked Steve, smiling. He was entertained at Mike's obvious unease. Regardless, he nuzzled back down into his jacket against the window.

Mike glanced his way twice while adjusting his position in the driver's seat. The deceitful silence filled back in the space and Mike relaxed back, peering out into the yellowed grey night.

He toggled the brights back on with his left foot and washed the trees along the roadside with that same eerie glow.

Here the median widened out to separate the east and westbound lanes.

"See ya tomorrow sunshine," Mike said as he made a grip in the air toward the yellow sign indicating a divided highway.

Steve lazily threw up the peace sign. It had been a tradition to acknowledge the split since day one; Mike's way of saying, "We're nearly halfway home."

Those kinds of traditions were common among friends. Scratch the ceiling if you pass under a yellow light. If it turned red while beneath it, Chamille suffered a punch to the headliner.

There were no streetlights out here though. The woods along I-40 east swallowed them up. The two traveled for the next fifteen minutes, like white noise, covered by that deceitful silence.

Chapter Two

"I loved you since I knew ya!
I wouldn't talk down to ya!
I have to tell you just how I feel
I won't share you with another boy..."

The radio had finally sent Mike some energy over the airwaves. He had cranked it up a bit.

The black hair that fell over his right eye allowed Mike to crush it when he really wanted to. Steve still couldn't help but laugh when he impersonated great singers.

"I know my mind is made up.
So put away your make up.
Told you once I won't tell you again
It's a bad way.
Roxanne!
You don't have to put on the red light!"

Mike twists the volume down just as Steve had started blushing. He then points out of the windshield, "Lookie here."

Steve could see the two infrared running lights tracing out the rhythm of the highway a half mile out ahead.

"We're catching them up," Steve said, now sitting upright in the newfound energy.

"They gotta be doing at least ninety," said Mike.

"Yeah, but we're catching them up."

Mike eyed the speedometer. The needle hovered at ninety-five.

Steve looked over at Mike. They were both still in their Zaxby's uniforms from their shift. They'd stayed after closing to filter the grease and smoke a spliff.

"You know they're gonna slow if they see our headlights. They're gonna think we're a cop coming up on 'em or something."

"Either way, we'll pass 'em eventually."

"What if it's the school bus?" Steve asked lowering the volume till the tunes were all the way gone.

Mike switched his hands on the wheel and pointed to the box of moon pies Steve had been hoarding, "How about handing me one of those?"

He snatched it greedily and tore the cellophane with his teeth.

"If that's that fucking ghost bus," Mike said taking a bite, "you'll see Chamille here do one-thirty."

The lights grew steadily as the two conveyances neared one another along that dark highway. Like events on a timeline.

Two sliders on a disk jockey's sound board, trying to find the right tune.

The old El Camino approached the other solo midnight traveler at the safe speed of seventy-five.

Steve was right, they had slowed in case it was cops catching up the rear.

"It's definitely not a cruiser," Mike said.

He nuzzled his Mr. Pibb into the cup holder on the dash.

"They're not all Crown Vics anymore," Steve said as they approached. "Jeff and I saw two Dodge Chargers fitted out with lights in Kingston Springs."

Mike flipped the blinker to indicate they'd be passing.

"It's nothing. See, no government tags."

"What is it a Chevelle?" Steve asked as they slid around the left rear bumper and out into the passing lane.

The windows were limousine tinted black, darker than Chamille's. No one was identifying anyone through those on either side. Especially on a night like this.

"A hatchback Chevelle?" scoffed Mike.

Her lines were dark. Pretty. All straights along the hind end. Tipped with points out over the chrome bumper.

"It's a hearse."

"Still, not as creepy as that bus," remarked Mike.

"You think they'd be down to race?"

"You kiddin' me? A hearse?" Mike reached over and snatched the straw from his fountain drink and stuck it in the corner of his mouth.

From a bird's eye view, the light of the headlamps floated along the surface of the night highway. Cones crisscrossing. The two cars would look like sliding dials, finally in tune.

Steve peered out of his tinted window into the darkness of the hearse's driver's side. Their own blackness reflected.

"Well they we're at least doing ninety back there. I mean," he gawked at Mike who was folding his straw in two, "I don't see any funeral procession."

Mike stuck the straw back in his mouth and looked over at the invisible driver floating along at seventy-five miles per hour.

"I don't know, but I got an idea."

"What?"

"You'll see."

Chapter Three

The two vehicles floated along the highway one right
next of the other. The clock on the dash dropped one of its
green LED sticks and the 9 on the 59 turned to a zero
making the time 12:00am.

Speed, seventy-five miles per hour.

"So, you're not gonna pass him?" asked Steve
adjusting his belt and stowing his jacket between them on
the bench.

"Uh, uh."

Mike reaches down and turns the music back up. Not
anything to grove to, just something unfamiliar. Ambient
sound.

Steve watched outside.

The dark window stayed right next to him as he
imagined the man inside staring back at him, who also
could not see.

Or could he?

Maybe he could see him. Maybe the tint on old
Chamille wasn't one hundred percent. Mike *had* said that
he didn't want her tinted so dark that it was illegal.

Steve couldn't remember ever being able to see
through from outside. At least not without cupping his
hands over his eyes really good. And it was dark out here
on the highway.

Well, those damn streetlamps gave off that strange
orange glow. Could that light be enough for the man behind
the one hundred percent tint to see his face? To see this
dimpled teenager grinning as his friend had a good time at
their expense?

There was time to think of all of that before Steve first noticed a change in pace.

They weren't racing but, Steve let out a sigh of relief when he realized Mike had let off the accelerator a little and decided to fall back. But no. It hadn't been that Mike had let off at all.

When Steve looked his way, Mike was gnawing on that straw like someone out of an old western. One hand draped over Chamille's steering column; eyes distant.

He knew that look. That was Mike's 'don't give a fuck' look. No, Mike hadn't let up at all.

It had been the other guy who had decided to speed up.

Steve rolled his head back over to the hearse and saw that Mike had evened up their windows again. The speedometer was rising above eighty. Still, no emotion from that obsidian dark. Just the chrome wheels, the passing white lines, and the invisible, nameless coachmen hidden behind dark glass.

Thirty seconds had passed and the speedometer steadily rose. Ninety, ninety-five.

'Oh, we're racing now!' thought Steve briefly, but that was being hopeful.

One hundred.

That's when something unexpected happened.

The hearse began to slow.

But so did Mike.

"What are you doing, we had 'em?" Steve said.

Mike just shook his head briefly refusing to look Steve's way. Gnawing.

It took only a minute to crawl back down to seventy-five. But the invisible coachmen's dark window still floated right outside of Steve's window.

"So, you're gonna just ride right beside him?"

"Uh huh."

Mike had that cold gaze. Laid back. Chewing. Focused.

Steve felt himself sink into the leather as Mike accelerated.

The hearse was off again, trying to break free of Mike's weird vice.

"Whoo hoo!" said Mike in a surprised voice. "They've got something under that hood."

From out of the front windshield, Steve could see Chamille's brown racing stripes that ran her body stem to stern. They disappeared over the maroon rim of the El Camino's hood. Right alongside that was the round eye of the driver's side headlamp of the hearse.

They were both barreling down the two-lane highway like an invisible tether connected them at the doors.

The speedometer crossed one-twenty. Then Steve's seat belt locked up as he pitched forward. The mysterious driver had slammed on the brakes in a desperate attempt to get from beside the El Camino. But Mike was flawless.

The needle dove to sixty miles per hour in less than three seconds. Still the opaque window remained flush, only three feet from Chamille's passenger door.

Then another forward pitch. Steve had expected rubber to melt on that one, but no.

Both cars dropped to thirty miles per hour. Twenty-five.

Then there was a bark from the hearse's rear tires as it dropped a gear and tried speeding off in escape. Led by its chrome hood ornament. Death and his sickle.

"There we go!" Mike said still starring forward. And the El Camino answered.

A billow of smoke chased both vehicles up the maddening highway. The hearse was now flashing his brights as the speedometers skyrocketed through one hundred again.

"You might get to see Chamille do one-thirty after all." Mike laughed. But he still chewed on that straw.

The engines roared. The high gear in both vehicles just then at that leveling whine where they can't possibly give anymore. Like a measuring tape pulled out to its maximum length.

"One-thirty!" Mike said, motioning with his wide eyes that Steve look at the speedometer.

Steve's ass was about as puckered as a sour starfish.

He was almost going to suggest Mike to lay off when the hearse took another nosedive. This time rubber left matching tracks a hundred yards.

Nose up.

Nose down.

Matchbox Twenty was playing in the speakers while they rode along on some seesawing carnival ride.

Sixty-five. Then ninety. Then fifty. Forty. Thirty. Twenty. Ten.

The hearse came to a complete stop, right there in the slow lane of I-40.

Steve looked at the window in the stillness. He could feel the tension behind that black safety glass. Under the music the idle of Chamille's motor was on high.

Mike had one foot on the brake and one on the gas; ready for anything.

Steve was tense as an overinflated balloon.

What if the guy gets out with a gun? Steve thought to himself. He wouldn't say anything though.

He just sat there staring in the dark, one hand gripping his shoulder belt, the other thumbing the miniature Swiss army knife clipped in his pocket.

Then suddenly Mike killed the music.

Steve turned his head and looked out of the back window. Saw nothing back there. Nothing ahead.

"Well," Mike said, "that's that, I guess."

Steve reached down in the floorboard and gathered up his jacket and moon pies. When he looked back up the brights on the hearse were flicking out three short bursts, then three long bursts, then three short bursts again.

S.O.S.

The message hadn't even registered when the old carcass hauler smoked its tires again. But Mike was on top of it.

Once more, they were barreling along out in the middle of nowhere. The needles on the dash climbing steadily. Mike gnawing on his straw, this time in silence.

Steve finally broke.

"Mike, you don't think—"

"Alright, alright!" barked Mike clearly annoyed with Steve trying to cutthroat his fun. He wasn't happy about it, but he was going to see reason.

Then, right before Mike lifted his foot off the accelerator, the hearse swerved.

The black death box veered into the El Camino's lane.

Steve watched in horror as the window that had floated next to him for nearly five adrenaline-filled minutes closed the gap in a heartbeat.

But Mike was fast and matched the move. He jerked the wheel left.

Chamille's tires barked and then sung like a giant hornet *BUZZ, BUZZ, BUZZ, BUZZ, BUZZ, BUZZ, BUZZ* along the sleeper lines at the edge of the emergency lane.

The fun had gone too far and Mike was finished with it. He mashed the brake.

'*Let them go on ahead*,' he thought.

But the hearse couldn't get any purchase. The back end swerved twice, wildly from right to left. Then like an off kilter top the ass end slid out from the left and a hub cap shot out into the woods.

Mike slowed further and the boys' breath caught in their throats as the great black hearse pitched and lost its front right tire off of the edge of the blacktop.

Steve's seat belt locked as Mike drove the brake into the floorboard, bringing Chamille to a complete stop.

Just out beyond the light of their headlamps, less than 500 yards away, the two boys witnessed the glass eyeballs of the hearse do somersaults and the brake lamps trace figure eights in the night like fireflies.

Through the silence came the scream of metal tearing and glass shattering and then the deafening sound of a giant striking a huge drum.

A cloud of grass and dust hung above the wreckage, the one operating headlamp trying to break through the thinning plume like the batman signal in the night.

Mike spit his straw in an absent attempt at the driver's side door pocket and leaned forward over the wheel, like a couple of inches would afford him a better look at what just happened.

Both boys knew the only way they were going to see any clearer was for the smoke to dissipate and for them to motor on up and have a look.

"Fuck, man," Steve whispered. He chanced a partial look over at Mike, trying his best not to be full of accusation, but it wasn't cool enough.

"What?!" Mike railed, "I didn't fuckin' touch 'em man! They wrecked themselves."

"I—I didn't say we did."

Mike swung his head full around to the rear and looked westbound out into the night. Silence.

Gently he lifted his foot from the brake and let Chamille begin to idle forward of her own accord.

"You think anyone'd survive that?" Steve asked, leaning too far into the windshield in an effort to look overly interested. Still trying to keep the guilt from falling too hard on his friend.

Chamille's tires walked out over the shards of safety glass, step by step. Her white walls obliterating a piece of bulb. Smoke curling up as the El Camino inched up beside the wreckage.

The hearse was on its roof. Passenger side crushed down. A and B posts flattened. It's where all the glass had come from. The windshield was spidered. Fractured in such a way the glass was a patchwork of white in the night.

Steve went to roll down his window but Mike had punched the window lock. When the window wouldn't budge, he looked back at Mike who was just shaking his head morbidly. Then, understanding, he looked back out at the slowly passing wreckage and heard Mike mutter, "They'll see our faces."

The under body was more like a truck than a car.

The exhaust pipe was full of grass and the catalytic converter was smoldering after something had melted onto it. The back door of the hearse was cocked open on a single hinge. Velvet drapery had been blasted from the interior out onto the shoulder. One piece was on fire, rolling along the emergency lane.

"You think they're okay?"

They were passing it at a crawl.

Mike put both hands on the wheel, checked the side views, and started gently accelerating away.

"I'm sure they are. But it's best not to find out."

As the undulating rhythm of Chamille's crankshaft went to work, Steve looked back from his window. The last thing he saw was the coffin on the other side of the ditch. It must've been pitched free in the crash. And the lid was missing.

Chapter Four

The radio's absence was thick, but welcome.

The deceitful silence filled the space for a full five minutes.

The green LEDs read 12:15.

Speed, seventy miles per hour.

Mike was the first to speak, "Do you think we should call it in when we get home?"

"Someone will stop before then. If we were in the Taurus we'd have the car phone."

Then Mike wondered, "Was there anyone in it?"

"Someone was driving."

"No. I mean the coffin. Was there anyone in the coffin?"

"Fuck it, Mike," Steve said balling up his jacket and stuffing it back in the crook of the door. "What's it matter? I mean, there might've been something. Who could even tell?"

Mike finally dared a look Steve's direction. It was the first time since motoring off. "You think we should have stopped?"

Steve answered from his corner. "I don't know what to think man. I don't want to think. What I want is a fuckin' drink."

Mike pointed to Steve's Pibb nestled in beside his own on the dash.

"You know what I mean!"

"Well," Mike said, "there's always that toxic Jell-O in the fridge we pulled on Jeff."

Steve sat up. "Yeah. Count me in on that shit. I'll eat the whole bowl!"

At least that conjured a weak smile from Mike. "Kevin'll be pissed if you get sloshed and don't show up to work tomorrow."

Steve saw the yellow sign that read 'CHECK GAS | NEXT EXIT TWENTY MILES' fly by in his peripheral vision, "You can tell Kevin I'm sick. Fuck it."

"Hell, I don't want to go in tomorrow either. But someone has to."

Mike shook his head, "Passing that spot again tomorrow night—" he met Steve's eyes across the bench seat, "—I don't know if I can handle it."

"Maybe we should take the next exit? Ya know, tell a store clerk we saw an accident."

Mike wasn't shaking his head this time. This time, he was just thinking. He ran the back of his right hand across his mouth.

"Nah. Our rubber is all over the highway back there. They gotta be able to match that to the tires or something."

He offered a feeble glance Steve's way, "Unless, you're insisting. If you're insisting. We'll do it."

Then he changed hands at the wheel and sulked under his own seat belt hanger. Clearly upset with himself.

Steve was just sitting there in silence. Considering. Just sitting there in that same deceitful silen—

What's that?

Up ahead, the four running lights of a trailer peaked out from the on-ramp of the last chance exit on I-40 East.

Mike sped up a little and toggled off the high beams. That helped Steve relax.

He'd made up his mind to just let the whole business of the crash go until they got home. Maybe a little spiked Jell-O *would* make things better.

The vehicle had merged straight into the fast lane.

Steadily they were closing the gap.

Approaching from the rear, the boys could make out the unmistakable dark metal eyebrows that covered the rear warning lights which would indicate following vehicles to stop for crossing children. Otherwise whitewashed, all four red lamps were aglow and in bold letters one could read EMERGENCY PULL TO EXIT and WE STOP AT ALL RR CROSSINGS along the back door.

"You gotta be shittin' me," Mike said coming up on her at eighty.

It wasn't a trailer after all.

White lines dashed beneath the El Camino's hood as they moved into the slow lane to pass.

Then there were those tinted windows. Eleven of them. Mike counted each double pane as he overtook her. Plus the bi-folding door panels. That made twenty-four, all rectangles, black as pitch.

The paint job was like sandstone. Matte, no gloss. Only a single chrome decal that read BLUEBIRD embossed into an upside-down Nike swoosh.

He eased off the accelerator to try and peer inside of the dark folding door.

No dice.

Steve startled him when he asked, "Prison transfer?"

"I... don't know," said Mike, uneasily.

Truth was, the whole thing was making him nervous. He was thinking about the people in the windows of that bus that was headed westbound early on. Before the whole ordeal.

"Coulda been prisoners," he said reluctantly.

The nose on the bus was old fashioned. It was a front-heavy with the long hood which housed the turbo diesel that

Mike could hear whistling now as the driver got onto the gas.

The El Camino nosed up to the front of the Bluebird's hood. Right to where Mike could see the passenger's side mudflap outside of the window.

It nosed up to it, but not past.

The green LEDs on the dash read 12:22.
Speed, eighty miles per hour.

Chapter Five

From above, four low beams crisscrossed along the moving slate. The two vehicles side-by-side along a dark channel like some blue whale with its baby.

All you could really see was the road.

Without the high beams on, you didn't get the full picture. The forest was still there. It was just a dark wood now.

Steve knew exactly what Mike was afraid of but he was still going to ask. Before he did, he reached down and volumed up the radio. The Police were singing Message in a bottle.

"C'mon man," Steve said, "What's there to worry about?"

Mike's stomach was turning to knots. He lifted his arm from blocking Steve's view of the instrument cluster and gave him that look again that said, 'Check it out.'

The needle was climbing through ninety and they weren't gaining any ground.

"I have a bad feeling, man," says Mike.

Beside them the diesel engine was swallowing air, and the front end of the Bluebird was gently bouncing under the strain of the transmission catching the final gear. Maximum overdrive.

Steve was bolt upright again holding onto the oh shit handle above his door. His grip was wet with his nervous sweat and he was wishing that this would all just go away.

The speakers mocked them as The Police sang their chorus,

I'll send an S.O.S to the world
I hope that someone gets my
I hope that someone gets my
I hope that someone gets my
Message in a bottle

"Fuck this," Mike said, "and kill that noise!"

Then he buried the gas pedal.

Chamille jumped like a racehorse just freed from its starting stall onto the track.

The double doors of the ghost bus held fast outside of the window.

For a moment Steve's heart dropped into his large intestine as he imagined all the bad karma coming their way.

But then, Chamille got a few inches on the Bluebird. Then a few feet.

They were pulling away!

He craned his neck around and looked into the front windshield of the bus. A dark strip of tint along the top prevented him from seeing the man's face, but Steve could see bony fingers in a death grip on the wheel, white with tension.

"I'm not stopping for anything," Mike squealed.

The dual exhaust below the El Camino rumbled away out in front of the bus which was disappearing into the dark.

Mike watched it go in the rear view.

Time 12:25.

Speed, one hundred and twenty-five miles per hour.

Chapter Six

The El Camino was thundering past mile marker two twenty-two when Steve finally asked Mike to consider easing off the gas.

"You know highway patrol likes to hide out in the woods by the Wilson County line."

It was true. They had avoided getting their licenses suspended for racing many times by cooling it near that speed trap.

Mike considered it. His eyes, bathed in a thinning band of white light, flicked up to the rear view and down at the speedometer. Nothing back there.

The reflectors atop the concrete barriers on the bridge were passing lighted stripes through the cab as they crossed over into Wilson County.

Mike had eased Chamille back down to around ninety but was reluctant to shy any more than that.

"C'mon Mike, just think about it. If the cops pull us over and ticket us, there's gonna be substantial evidence tying us to the wreck. It'll put us along this highway right at the time of the accident."

Mike's eyes canvased the stretch of dark behind them. Again, he looked beneath his hand at the gauges.

"Ah shit, man!" said Steve.

A pair of blinding headlights had flicked on from the wooded crossover path connecting the east and westbound lanes. It was precisely where they had gotten lucky time and time again.

It seemed; their luck had run out.

The El Camino lulled forward as Mike's foot fell off the accelerator in an attempt to get within twenty over. He didn't need a reckless driving charge.

Steve put his head back against the bench seat, looking up at the headliner.

"I told you."

Now, the patrolman was easing out from the forest onto the deserted highway. It's headlamps rocking as the tires gained purchase on the asphalt.

No blue lights yet, though.

Something about those headlamps.

They weren't any kinda lights they had ever seen on an interceptor before.

Come to think of it. Mike got a strange feeling about the way those bright lights came on firsthand. Not very police-like, he thought. It felt more like he were in a dirty harry movie and some gangsters were lying in ambush for him.

That's what those lights reminded him of, an old-fashioned car from a Dirty Harry flick.

Mike pressed on the gas.

"What are you doing?" asked Steve in desperation. "You can't outrun a cop!"

"If that's a cop then I'm Shirley Temple," said Mike.

Steve looked back, shielding his eyes with his right hand.

"It's blacker than the road. And they haven't made a police car shaped that way since the nineteen forties."

Steve was still trying to make it out from so far back. He didn't like those headlights. They were making him feel like he was living in one of the scary stories to tell in the dark. He was a frightened little kid again.

The truth was, he hadn't seen headlamps like those except on early model cars. And the last time he'd seen such an early model car, it had been upside down, shining its only good lamp up through a plume of dirt and dust.

The green LEDs read 12:28.
Speed, one hundred miles per hour.

"How much further before the exit?"

Steve pointed to the green mile marker blazing past on the right. Mile 225.

"Should be less than ten miles from here."

That was according to the yellow sign Steve remembered that had said NEXT EXIT TWENTY MILES.

Behind them the high beams on the old car that neither Steve nor Mike chose to name, began flashing. It still hadn't closed any distance since Mike chose to keep on the gas, but the message was one they'd grown far too familiar with that night. It was Morse code.

Even though neither of the boys vocalized their belief that it was the death box behind them again, they both knew it amid the blinding SOS through their rear window. However, both boys were pretty confident they'd make the exit.

At least until Chamille guttered.

What else had that yellow sign said?

The massive round speedometer that took up the whole center of the instrument panel showed the El Camino's speed steadily dropping.

Over in the left-hand corner of the cluster, where some of the smaller gauges hid, a less conspicuous needle rested on the peg below 'E'.

That was the fuel gauge.

"Mike?"

The speed was plummeting. Ninety-five. Ninety.

The globular lenses were closing the gap behind them, now.

Eighty-five.

"Mike, we're sitting ducks, man!" Steve's face had gone all flush under his pimples. It was so red you could hardly tell they were there.

Mike was trying to ignore the incessant flashing. Blinded by every other flick of the brights.

He pushed the column shifter to neutral. The RPMs dropped to zero.

The Camino continued to coast. Eighty. Seventy-five. Seventy.

He reached over in front of Steve and pinched the catch on the glove box. It fell open, spilling out a mix of documentation and Zaxby's condiments.

"In the back," he said, "there's a metal switch for the reserve."

Steve dove into the glove compartment. Clearing out all the clutter in one or two big grabs.

The dark nose of their pursuant was tearing toward them now like they were standing still. Its pretty lines were unmistakable. The sharp points. The chrome hood ornament.

Chamille coasted at sixty. Mike felt totally helpless when the hearse's left blinker came on indicating it would pass.

'Fat chance,' Mike thought.

He looked over and saw that Steve had stopped what he was doing to watch the hood ornament, a chrome grim reaper, slide up cooly along the driver's side.

"Steve! For God's sake," Mike screamed, "the reserve!"

Steve's hand had just happened across it. He twisted it to tank B.

Chapter Seven

Time, 12:30.
Speed, Fifty miles per hour.

The stretch of interstate before the two eastbound vehicles reminded Steve of a haunted house. Those you enter into and the strobe lights make everything look like its moving slower than it actually is.

The impossible hearse was flicking out its SOS while Mike was pumping the gas pedal and turning the ignition. Her own lights sputtered with the reel of the starter motor.

The woods along the left side of I-40 passed in long bright swaths and then quick intermittent light.

The trees and gutter along the right side flicked to the tune of the ignition relay. In one flicker Steve saw a gnarled tree jutting from the embankment on the right. Then another time the eye shine of a racoon or possum at the edge of the woods.

But the strobe of the lights wasn't exactly deceiving them. They *were* slowing!

Forty miles per hour. Like a snail drying up from underneath. Thirty-five.

Then she caught a spark.

Mike's foot was still mashing the gas to prime her when she fired and Chamille's motor roared through eight thousand RPMs. When the hammer dropped into drive the chassis nearly twisted under the torque.

She made a low bellow from the rear wheels but grabbed the road. Her bench seat hugged both Mike and Steve who felt like they were jumping a horse over an obstacle. Then she was off. The maddening invisible coachman on their left answering in his own terrible anthem.

When the Camino's lights came back on steady, the glare of the silver grim reaper mocked them from the hood of the other conveyance. Thrusting its scythe out as if already in victory.

A cloud of dark soot roiled behind the vehicles after the hearse's driver buried his accelerator and with some ungodly power, lifted the front tires several inches from the highway.

Steve had cinched his seat belt down with his left hand. The box of moon pies was crushed under his right non-slip work boots, still caked with grease. He didn't notice.

Steve started pleading with Mike as the needle rose and the hearse remained stationary beyond the driver window.

Just darkness. Just the feeling of impending doom and darkness.

"Mike, please!"

"Look!" Mike pointed with his eyes, "the exit!"

It was out there. The big green sign read, EXIT 235 ONE MILE.

Mike just couldn't concentrate from all the incessant lights flicking out that damn Morse code. **SOS. SOS. SOS.**

It was blinding him.

Steve closed his eyes, scared to the point of wanting to punch his friend in the chest if it would only make him stop accelerating. But the exit, it was there! If only another thirty seconds.

Mike had had enough. He flicked on his own bright lights with his left foot to drown out the flashing.

Steve opened his eyes.

And there it was. Like it had been for millions of others before them.

Death.

Chapter Eight

First it was the eye shine of the young doe. Then the two fawns crossing behind her in the slow lane.

"Shi—" Mike's voice caught in his throat. Though later Steve would think it was sucked out of him with the vacuum of the imploding cabin.

The front wheels had turned toward the emergency lane. Chamille disputed. Rubber melted in the rear as Mike's feet pounded the brake.

She fishtailed. He thought he had her. But the front right tire lost the roadway and she went up in a figure eight. Racing stripes along her nose screw driving into the dirt.

There was glass. Tearing metal. Even the sound of a giant hitting a drum. But this time Steve was inside of it all.

Outside, the dust was rising through the high beam which was twisted in an angle to spotlight the trees.

There was a bulb just outside of the passenger side window, laying on the concrete in the slow lane. It was still flickering with the last life of electricity though most of its housing had been shorn away.

Steve turned his head to Mike as he himself hung upside down, suspended from Chamille's bench seat.

There was no Mike. Only a crushed A and B post, a twisted steering wheel. An empty seat.

He'd been thrown free.

It made him think of the lidless coffin he'd seen on the side of the freeway and his reluctance to tell Mike what he'd seen inside.

Chamille's engine had died. It's fuel filter giving up pumping against gravity. There was silence, besides the distant rumble of an interested and onlooking motorist.

The death box.

Then, like something from a dream, he heard the hearse's motor idle slowly forward. Safety glass was cracking and popping under the weight of the hearse as it eerily advanced.

The gray freeway became lighter and lighter in its head lamps, glittering with a thousand tiny diamonds of safety glass shrapnel.

Finally, a tire rolled over the large flickering bulb in the slow lane and made a resounding *POP*.

Then it stopped right outside of Steve's window.

Steve forced in a breath. His right arm might still be good. Not good enough to unbuckle the seat belt. And even if he could, God he didn't think he could take the drop to the headliner. He tried for his buckle anyhow.

No use, plus he felt paralyzed from the waist down.

The engine on the hearse went silent and then Steve could make out the slowing whine of one of Chamille's tires still spinning.

Must be rubbing on a bent wheel well.

He forced another breath and held it. It was like inflating a hot water bladder. He could feel the sweat rolling down his scalp and dripping, but when he looked beneath him, the headliner was soaked in blood.

Steve was dying.

Back in the Banyan

When a heavy, shadow blotted out the light inside of Kristen's hideout, she raised her chin from her creative writing journal where she'd been dedicating an entire page to the sketch of the Grim reaper, but the light returned as quickly as it threatened to go.

She glanced over her shoulder at the entrance.

"Birds," came the Reaper's voice from below, before she could even consider what it may have been.

Kristen put her chin down onto her wrists. She had crossed them over her artwork and was looking back down into the old storeroom of weird stuff.

"So, they hit a deer?"

The Skeletal thing was still holding that hood ornament in his hand like he was remembering something from his own past or something.

"Many times," he said.

Kristen face wrinkled up in confusion.

"Do you know what this world's deadliest animal is?" asked Death hoarsely.

For some reason Kristen thought she knew what he would say, but it made no sense.

"Not humans," the skull remarked. "Deer," he then said simply, swinging the ornament so that the tiny sickle made an imitation of lopping off someone's head.

Kristen lay her head over to one side.

"Deer?"

"Well, perhaps they can also be called the bravest animals." He looked thoughtful, well, as thoughtful as one could look without eyebrows anyhow. "Though," Death continued, "Cecil would say that you can always substitute the trait of bravery with stupidity."

"Who's Cecil?" she asked.

"No one of consequence. Just a Twit I was growing rather fond of. But you know what they say about Twits."

He could see clearly that she didn't.

"They know their statistics," he said. "If not for the stupidity and or bravery of the deer, the mortality rates of motor vehicle collisions would be negligible."

Death looked back at the hood ornament, "There's also the whole deer-in-the-headlights thing, as well."

Kristen often wondered if hypnosis might help her get over the loss of her dad like it had helped her mom get over smoking.

When Death looked back to her, it was past the ornament he was holding aloft in her direction. She could see those coins in his eyes doing their little random spinning trick. Flashing grey and white in no certain gait that could be followed.

She watched the lights do their random spinning and felt like a cowboy trying to break a horse that was bouncing along at some unimaginable canter.

First, it bucked. Then it did a two and three-step hoof beat, and then a four. Then back to a two and three-step hoof beat, and then a two-step again. She was getting tired and couldn't figure out the cadence, but the horse wasn't tiring at all. It just kept right on doing all that fancy stepping.

She felt that if she could just figure out the pattern of those hooves then she could ride smoothly and then, then she could master the beautiful animal. But if she couldn't then she might…

"The deceitful silence," Death said, bringing her back to the story.

She had been daydreaming.

"Yes, it can fool you. Lull you to sleep, while reading a book, or riding shotgun in your friend's El Camino after a long night of work.

"Those underlying audible rhythms that can hypnotize you while driving a long familiar highway. They can be deadly.

"Steve wished he was being deceived. Wished he could close his eyes and nod off to the road noise now. But, when the rubbing of the El Camino's warped wheel finally came to a stop, another insistent sound kept him from shutting his eyes and pretending it was all a dream.

"He even forced another painful breath as a diesel engine approached the scene. It pulled off the shoulder in front of the accident. The compression brakes hissed as the vehicle came to a stop. But Steve was no idiot. And this was no emergency response vehicle," Death said, his eyes finally releasing her from their magnetism and returning to the hood ornament.

"*That* was the sound of a white Bluebird bus that had finally caught them up."

Chapter Nine

The whitewashed bus went quiet, then dieseled for a moment, then died.

Steve felt a lot like the motor he was hearing, when from under the hearse he could see a dingy sneakered footstep out from the driver's side and meet the pavement.

What he saw made him catch a short second wind.

Toes were bursting through the obliterated canvas of the size-fifteen shoe.

Then, another yellow toe-nailed appendage joined it before the hearse went from a low rider to a two-foot clearance among the squealing relief of the leaf springs.

Then Steve could see pant legs rising above the columns which were the man or beast's hairy ankles. The pants were prison-inmate orange.

Steve sucked wind in short gasps and tried again for the seat belt clasp. He couldn't get his hand up that high, so he settled for the hem of his work pants and started trying to pull his legs from under the dash, hoping the weight might break him free. It was a desperate attempt.

The glass between the Camino and the hearse started going ape shit. It was being pounded by a hundred hammers. His head was a mess of blurred vision and tinnitus. Then, clearly, just outside of his window, a dozen cloven hooves danced in between the two cars.

He was paralyzed again with fear as images of the devil, the minotaur, and every other evil being flashed before his eyes. But then the family of hooves stopped stock still like… deer in the headlights.

That's when he remembered the face of death on the road and a riddle about the deadliest animal on the planet.

But Steve had no clue what the true face of death looked like. Not yet.

There was still breath in his lungs.

"Get out of here!"

A baritone but raspy voice demanded as the car door slammed on the hearse.

Steve's arm dropped to shield his eyes from the glass that the hooves kicked up wildly as they retreated.

One deer, the big one, collided side long into the overturned El Camino and the slight rock shifted Steve's feet out from under the dash.

Greasy and mushed moon pies rained down around him. And then he saw red as the seat belt bore all his weight into his already separated shoulder.

He couldn't take the fall to the headliner, but he couldn't breathe at all like this. Folded in half, like some kind of discarded rag doll.

Two enormous metal clangs brought Steve's attention outside of the window.

"Open up!" it was the Giant again. But it was coming from up by the Bluebird.

The bus door swooshed open with a *CLACK* just as Steve saw the glint of his Swiss army knife resting right outside of the window.

It must've come free when his feet dropped.

However it happened, it was there. He reached. But, his brain felt like their midnight race with the hearse. The blood vessels were pounding out the miles per hour. Skyrocketing through the nineties.

He heard the groan of the bus's shocks as the Giant climbed up a step.

His fingertips brushed the key ring on the pocketknife. *Just... out... of... reach.*

The Bluebird's shocks sighed in relief as the giant stepped back out of the doorway and his footfalls began lumbering off in the opposite direction. But another pair of feet had joined the party. The bus driver's, and they were shuffling his way.

He stopped struggling; defeated. Breathless. His hand dropping helplessly back into the disaster that was the Camino's roof.

The sandaled feet that slid their way through the shimmering safety glass toward him were nothing but bone. Skeleton's. Like a plastic cast you'd see in science class. Except these were held together by hairlike musculature.

The feet came, then after only a brief pause, when Steve had shut his eyes, they turned and moved on toward the back of the hearse.

He opened his eyes and there, resting among the shit covered moon pies, was Mike's straw. Chewed to a mangled and stiff little stick.

Steve forced his diaphragm to respond one last time and snatched the straw from the mess. The vessels in his head topped one-thirty, but he hooked the key ring and claimed the Swiss.

The back door of the hearse whined as it opened on its long side hinge and Steve pictured the overturned vehicle they'd left behind and the door ajar in that same unique way. But it didn't stop him from popping the blade out with his thumb and starting in at the nylon disappearing into the base of the door frame.

His head was a pulsing water balloon filled with boiling water. His teeth were being ground to nubs as he sawed.

Alongside his efforts the giant had returned, and his massive sneakers crushed huge ignorant steps of wreckage as they passed between the hearse and the Camino.

And then he'd done it!

The belt came free and Steve piled down onto the roof. He would have screamed had he the wind, but instead, as he unfolded semi-prostrate he welcomed a huge swallow of air and rolled sideways. His hand resting just outside of the voided window.

Now he could see the rear tires of the death box. The two mawing sneakers were standing to one side and the skeleton's feet were positioned to draw something out of the cargo space. It took a few steps back and the rollers under the casket whistled.

Then a voice like a woodwind instrument came.

"You can never warn them, Carl."

A stand swung down in front of the Reaper's black robes, propping up the casket like a makeshift pall bearer. Then the lid was lifted and the giant inmate un-shouldered something into the box.

There is no description for the sound of a dead body being dropped into a coffin.

Steve just watched the under body of the hearse rock and the casket-stand slightly shift. His jaw was languid. Permanently fixed in an open position, resting on his shoulder. Drooling...

But his eyes still saw everything.

"You can't warn them," came the woodwind voice again, "and you can't save them."

Then, Steve could imagine the giant freak closing the lid on the coffin with his right hand when he heard a *CLAP,* and then he saw the coffin-stand lifted by the brute's other hand before the odd couple's feet guided his friend Mike's final resting place into the back of the Reaper's death box.

The hearse's rear door shut, and Steve remembered that coffin lying on the other side of the ditch. It had been missing its lid and it had been full alright.

Chapter Ten

How long since he had taken a breath?
A minute? Maybe two?

The Swiss army knife was still resting in the joints of his last three fingers. He curled them up around the red. That's when the cold steel of an iron shackle captured his wrist outside of the window.

The brute braced himself with a massive foot against the car's side panel, the sheet metal denting under the weight. Another foot twisted for better purchase just beyond Chamille's door frame and then the length of chain attached to the ring around Steve's wrist went tight, drawing him out of the window like a puppet.

It was terribly unforgiving. Numbing. Like stubbing a toe, but this was his other helpless shoulder. There was nothing he could do but hold tight his grip on his measly one-and-a-half-inch dirk.

The bloated inmate tossed Steve up in the air and bear hugged him like a child with an old doll. Steve's lumbar region screamed as he found himself staring into the face of a fleshy Frankenstein.

When the giant began toward the Bluebird's open door, it was as if one oversized rag doll were carrying another.

Was this the invisible coachman? A heavy footed, doughy eyed, mockery of humanity? An inmate from hell's yard?

Steve was gazing over its shoulder, mindlessly counting the black windows of the Bluebird as Mike had once done. Then they reached the door and Carl (If such a thing like this could have a name!) twisted Steve like a weightless dummy in his grip. Carrying him feet first underarm like a blow-up doll.

That's when he saw the full view of the terrifying scene.

Chamille, belly-up on the shoulder, just as they'd left the hearse not twenty miles back. Something on fire rolling like a tumble weed along the edge of the emergency lane toward them. The hearse, parked half in the slow lane half in the emergency lane. And coming, drifting toward them along the stone white half-hallway of the Bluebird, a Grim Reaper.

How long since he'd taken a breath?

To be seeing what he was seeing.

A wraith. Flowing dark canvas full of hollows that held nothing but bone. Bone that held nothing but his scythe and inside the hollows of the bones themselves, there was a dim light that threatened.

Light in those eye sockets that said, "Look closer."

But the spell was broken when Carl hoisted him through the doorway and up the steps of the Bluebird. There was no air to scream when he met his fellow travelers.

Shackled along the sides were eleven men and five women. To describe them would be to lessen the horror which Steve felt. Though, he was beyond physical pain. Another pain filled the void. Like that deceitful silence of the road once had done.

It was full of faces just like his whose reflections he made out only through the inside windowpanes they faced. Gaping jaws, toothless. Skinless. Some eyes absent, lidless.

Deflated breasts lying along a rib cage, skin the color, and he imagined the texture of petrified wood. Yet the fingers moved. All mostly naked.

Was he naked now?

Nothing. He couldn't turn his head to see. No response from his motor functions, but for that one hand that still gripped the dirk. And as Carl, his behemoth host, pushed him forward through the row toward the back, he reached with it.

The Specter that was Death had taken the driver's seat already when the sound of nails on a chalkboard tore through the Bluebird's innards.

The blade was to the windows, tearing the tint in a screaming admonition of a dead friend's memory, until it caught in one of the aluminum trimmings and the pocketknife was torn from his frozen hand.

He was forced to the sixth window on the driver's side alongside five other unfortunate souls. The nearest, a mess of jaundiced skin sagging in folds and riddled with pinkish welts. But he saw *that* large man out of his peripheral vision. In front, his eyes stared through the tear in the tinting and out across the eastbound lane of I-40 to the dark woods.

A huge hand was between his shoulder blades which had finally surrendered their pain. It was pressing him to the wall while his left hand was shackled, then the length of chain attached to his right was fed through a metal eyelet and pulled tight.

No feeling in all of this. No way to watch it, but he knew by the domino sound of the chain jackhammering through and the way his wrists took the weight of his limp body.

Steve's head nodded onto his right shoulder, his mouth still gaping in that same frozen look of dread as when he'd struck the El Camino's headliner.

How long since he'd taken a breath?

He thought of Mike in the darkness of his coffin and envied him.

Steve's eyelids now would not respond. They were stuck open, staring. His eyeballs would dry up, not unlike these other twitching corpses, and probably rot away.

There'd be darkness then.

How long would it take for the sound to go away?

The memories?

Perhaps he should have taken a closer look when death had dared. For now, it seemed he'd stumbled across something worse than death.

The whole bus rocked back and forth and with it, Steve's corpse swayed away and to. The behemoth was lumbering his way back up the isle toward the exit.

Two creaks as it took the steps. The passengers were only aware that the Bluebird had regained its proper stature after losing Carl's weight because their personally permanent sceneries came to rest.

Then Death reached a bony hand over and grasped the handle of the door lever.

"Carl," it said through stone vocal cords, "don't try and warn them, Carl. You're just wasting your time."

"What else is there to do?" asked the Juggernaut.

"Well then," Death sighed. "Suit yourself."

Then he pulled the lever and the obsidian doors snapped tight.

There was a low vibration through Steve's corpse as the Grim Reaper turned the ignition and got the Bluebird in gear. Then the scenery started sliding by as they drove.

The whitewashed Bluebird took the exit and stopped at the four way as the moon reached its apex in the sky. Death reached over to the dash and picked up his shades with bony fingers.

"Well, boys and girls, it's a full moon tonight!"

Then he flipped on the radio, put his sunglasses over his eyes (to keep out the light; or was it to keep it in?), then flicked on the left turn signal and gave her some diesel.

The bus crossed under the overpass and took the left onto I-40 westbound back toward Music city.

Steve's not-so-personal ferry across the river Styx had a awfully familiar feel to it. As the scenery flew by, first of nothing but trees, and then to wear the highway came together again, he was accompanied by the deceitful silence of the road.

And in the speakers the Police were singing.

I'll send an S.O.S to the world
I hope that someone gets my
I hope that someone gets my
I hope that someone gets my
Message in a bottle

Funny thing was. For a brief moment, he thought he saw a maroon El Camino with brown stripes and dark tint pass them going eastbound.

The Father of Lies and the Fickle Finger of Fate

The grim reaper was tired of holding the hood ornament, besides the girl up there had seemed to have lost interest.

"Just to think. They thought it was safer to carpool," he said experimentally.

No response.

"Death seemed to agree," he said.

Still nothing.

"Ah em!"

Kristen had been sitting with her back to the brick wall while she was doodling, just listening to the creepy death thing rattle off the rest of his tale when she thought she heard him clear his throat. Which begged the question.

Did he even have a throat? What other body parts must he be missing?

She rolled back onto her tummy and peered through the hole at him again.

"So, is it better to carpool or isn't it?" Kristen asked turning her hand over in a motion of question and making the bunny part of her ink pen stick out to the side. She must've looked like a total ditz to Death from down there. Thinking that might be so, she owned it and stuck her other pinky in the corner of her mouth doing her best to blush.

"Better for the environment," Death said, adjusting his robes awkwardly.

She wondered if he could get a, you know, under that cloak. She put the question in her writing book. Then stole a quick glance back down at the freaky thing and added below it:

My God, I've seemed to dodge the perverts and ended up with a perfectly respectable skeleton and it's my mind in the gutter! That's exactly why Mom doesn't want me hanging out with the boys all of the time. Whatever. You think of these things when dudes are made up of nothing but bones!

Then she closed the notebook and slapped the pen down on top of it.

"So, what's with the shoe?" she asked the Reaper.

Death reached below the table to where Kristen finally noticed a blue and white wicker hamper. His skeleton fingers tipped the lid back and he threw the hood ornament forcefully into it causing a brief flash of light to emanate from within before the lid clapped back down.

Death dusted his hands together as if being rid of some soiled napkin. If he had possessed any lips, they would have smacked.

"Now, where were we?"

"The shoe," Kristen said with renewed interest.

"Oh, yes."

Death, reached over and took his sickle from the pile of old rubbish where Kristen had forgotten all about it. She could hear the tocking of the wooden tip on the floor as he walked step by step toward her. She edged back a little, despite him being a good ten feet down there in the basement.

The sun was now directly above the giant banyan, so the inside of the chamber was considerably dimmer.

"Don't be afraid, Kristen."

Besides the fact that the thing she was talking with was a skeleton, she was smart enough to realize that he could easily reach her with that long and deadly sickle if he chose to. Plus, she had heard what happens if you are touched by Death. She wasn't entirely sure if that counted for objects he was holding in his hand but felt it a pretty sure bet that his sickle would do the same trick, and in more ways than one!

"How do I know I can trust you?" she asked the thing.

"I told you," he said in that woodwind baritone of his. "It isn't your time. Besides, I would never lie. I am the incarnation of Death, not the Devil!"

"You mean the Devil is real, too?" Kristen cried.

Geesh. She was only just starting to doubt Santa Clause. She'd been reasonably certain that the Easter bunny was a hoax, but now she couldn't know what to think!

The Reaper seemed to be peering off into the cave, which Kristen couldn't see from this angle. He looked contemplative.

Kristen could hardly stand the silence.

"Well?" she demanded. "I just thought our parents made that up to scare us!"

Death turned his head up to her so she could look into the silver flicker of his sockets again and she knew what he said was true. The Devil would be as real as Death. Just because the Reaper told her that it wasn't her time, didn't mean that her time would never come.

The same must be true of Satan!

"Don't fear the father of lies, child," The skull said to her through its emotionless stare. Yet, the inflection had a bit of sympathy in it. "But be wary of his temptations. It is easy to be tricked by the scoundrel."

Death thought better than telling her his real purpose here, but the girl was kind of growing on him. Besides, Fate hadn't forbade him to do anything so specific…

"In fact," he said to Kristen, "You and I are here because Fate herself is attempting to remedy a bargain the Devil tricked her into."

Kristen wasn't sure she could wrap her head around all of this. If Death's persona looked like a skeleton, she wondered what the Devil's would look like, or furthermore, what Fate's would resemble.

"You mean Fate is real, too!"

She briefly tried to think of any other strange beings that she may be missing and then gave it up.

"I think you know the answer to that. Well, let's just say when it comes to the fickle fingers of Fate. *Her* fingers, that is. I do as directed.

"You can't blame her. I mean, what's a girl to do when the loom is running out of thread? God wouldn't intervene. Only way to keep weaving the very fabric of reality was to do the unmentionable."

"Do you mean," Kristen said blithely, "make a deal with the Devil? She really did it?"

"And I'd guess you would do it too if you found yourself at the end of your line," said Death.

She considered this.

"The only way Fate could obtain another spool, of the universal variety, was to promise the Devil that she would pull some strings and have Time killed before he botched Satan's only successful attempt at altering the future."

She was jotting down the incarnations in her creative writing journal. She added Time to the list. "So, the Devil altered the future?"

"Will, alter the future. Yes"

"Why?"

"To unbalance the power of good and evil into his favor."

"And this 'Time' foiled his plan?"

"Correct. Uh, *will*, foil his—"

"will foil his plan," she finished for him, "Yes, yes. Unless we—" she stopped abruptly, then said, "Wait! So what you are meaning to tell me is that we aren't just metaphorically killing Time here, but that you mean to literally kill him?"

He grinned. "We call him Chronos."

"Isn't that wrong? The devil balancing the power into his favor? I mean, can't you just say that you refuse?"

"We'll just say that Fate has me whipped. I mean she is the most attractive of the incarnations, after all."

Then, he put a bony phalange to his chin and tapped it a few times thoughtfully. "Actually, Mother Nature, is pretty too. But, only in certain seasons."

She rolled back over to her bottom and slumped back against the brick again.

What in the heck would all this mean? Was she going to cease to exist when this went down, or what? Oh, now she was wishing she would have just gone to school like she was supposed to.

She heard what sounded like Death shuffling his feet down there, so she looked over her shoulder at him and saw that was exactly what he was doing! He was prodding at a yoyo with his bleach white metatarsals. Playing with it, so that it rolled to and fro.

"Are you... are you bored?!" she exclaimed, totally fed up with the old deadhead.

He looked casually back up at her.

"Well, we still have a few hours before Chronos will arrive."

"Ugh! You're impossible!" she huffed, then went back to sulking.

Just then, she heard a raspy croak from outside of her tree fort. She stood up and wandered to the opening she had made in the roots and vines and looked outside. After her eyes adjusted to the bright light, she saw that a huge black raven had lit atop the old covered well. Its head was jerking to one side and then the other as fast as its eye would blink and she could tell that it was trying to get a clear look at her.

For some reason, it made her feel nervous, so she ducked back under the protective cover of the ancient roots.

"There's a black bird out there," she finished saying as she came close to the little window again.

She was straining to see down into the cavern after all of that bright light outside and finally began making out the shape of the old, dilapidated shoe in Death's weathered grip.

"I'm not surprised," said Death. "The Dark One's minions are everywhere. It's likely he just wants to be sure that Fate carries out her part of the bargain, or else there will have to be a trial."

"A trial?" asked Kristen. "You mean, like a judgement before God?"

"Something like that, but a bit more computerized," Death said wearily.

"I mean, couldn't God just, you know. Poof the old Devil away or something?"

She thought she saw Death actually yawn. His jaw moved side to side a little, and she could swear she heard an echoey woosh somewhere in her head.

"Am I," then giving him a disgusted look, "boring you?"

"It's just I've been overworked lately, is all," he said. Then his hand holding the shoe by the heel dropped to his side like he was giving up talking about the shoe for a moment.

"It's like this, okay," he said reluctantly. "God is under a strict contract of non-intervention. If you think about it, he represents all things loving and faithful and if he went around changing things as he pleased, he wouldn't be showing a whole lot of faith in the way things will turn out now would he?"

Kristen's corneas went to the corners of her eyes for a moment and then she smiled and huffed a sigh of relief.

"See there!" she said spryly, "Now was that so hard?"

"No," he said, but something told her he was just being agreeable. Then he lifted the shoe back up hopefully.

"And don't worry about Chronos," he said with renewed confidence, "He'll soon remember that we're doing him a favor. I could kill him literally if I wanted to you know. But I was never one to take what the Devil says too seriously. I have a feeling that the Father of Lies may soon learn that he shouldn't take what Fate says too seriously, either.

"But beware, Kristen. The Father of Lies doesn't take kindly to being outsmarted. Expect him to be a little, eh hem, heated. So, be about your wits when you leave, will you?"

She nodded, feeling a bit hopeful, but also a bit nervous.

"Allow me to put your mind at ease for a bit," said Death looking through the ankle of the shoe and out through the missing toes at her. "This next story was written by a girl your own age. Like you, this seventeen-year-old also thought it might be her time, to, what was it you wanted to ask me? Bite the big one?"

Kristen had forgotten all about that and was entirely sure she did not want to know specific dates anymore.

"Let's just say, you have plenty of time ahead of you if you keep your wits about you. Tanner's story may help you see that things and people, as much as they look like one thing for certain, may not be exactly what they seem."

Death's eyes went all hypnotic again, and Kristen thought she could indeed imagine a girl her age jotting things in her own creative writing notebook. Then his voice turned from that hollow echo inside of her head, to the voice of a teenager beginning to recount…

TANNER AND THE HAMPER OF HORRORS
Chapter One

Right around when I turned thirteen, the girl began.

I'd gotten into the world's worst habit of leaving my dirty clothes on the bedroom floor.

So, sue me, right?

Mom had started to take notice when she found Gabe, that's my baby brother, rolling around in a pile of my dirty underwear. Mom had also noticed then that I had a disproportionate number of thongs at that point in my life.

Could our relationship have been any more strained?

Around that time, Dad tripped over a pair of my stretch pants one morning. He was quick to remind me that I was not too old for a spanking. Had anyone been staying over that night I may have literally died from embarrassment at the comment.

I guess it was all amusing to Gabe because he laughed from his crib. I'd have punched the little terd If he wasn't two. Instead, he gets the tongue. A child-friendly version of flipping the bird.

If Gabe were telling the story he'd be all like, "Tanner almost got a spay spay from Dada!"

Not then though, he'd still be blubbering.

Don't ask me why I baby talk with my little brother. Maybe Mom did me that way.

Not to worry, there won't be much of that in this story. I'm seventeen now, and my dad's a writer. I'd just like to leave behind a little something for my baby brother to remember me by.

Besides, this story is not for babies, but he'll appreciate it when he's old enough to read it. If it doesn't scare him half to death!

You're gonna say that some things in this story sound like a load of crab. And well, somethings were a total load of crap! You'll agree when we get there. But I'm gonna tell it like it happened and I won't elaborate too much. Dad says that's how amateurs write.

The main thing is, when Gabe reads this, I just want him to know how much I loved him and will always love him.

One day, about at the point in my teenage life that I decided I'd been paying my dues far more than I'd been enjoying myself, Mom must've been out shopping for secondhand clothing.

I say that because, that was when she came home with 'the thing'.

I was at school that afternoon so I can only tell you how I think it likely went with her. Even though, I can be mostly sure of the details because later in that strange week, I personally came to know the store that my mom ended up in.

The shop was one of those jobs with stained glass windows, featuring more cracks, than rod iron. Mom liked those kinds of dives; homes converted into places of business. She called it the Art District. I called it the ghetto.

Back before Gabe, when mom used to paint a lot, I would steal the Mardi Gras beads off of the pilings out front of those places while mom shopped for antique frames.

That kinda gives a picture of the district. Seawall pilings in driveways, topped with moldy pelican statues. Not the proper ones, but the skinny ones that you'd have a hard time telling if they were plastic or real cement.

Who'd ever heard of a skinny pelican?

Inside the shop, Mom would be riffling through the clothes hangers, already having decided that she wanted the cursed thing she had found. She never starts flipping through clothes until she's cased the good stuff.

"What a great selection of children's clothes you have here," she'd say.

To which the lady of the shop would reply, "Thank you, Dear."

You can imagine teeth like bacon grease and splinters, she is the antagonist after all.

"A lot of things fall into my lap around these parts. Do you see anything you like?" she'd ask.

"Actually, I am most interested in this wicker piece over here. How much for the hamper?"

You see? That's how Mom rolls.

It was then that the crone would've looked at her with one milky eye and replied, "Oh, I couldn't charge you for that old thing. If you like it you can have it for free."

And here you might say that sounds like a heap of crap, but I am telling you now, milky eye? Yes. I know, because later, I was there. And we will get to that!

In fact, I've always referred to the old witch that owned that shop as Mrs. Partridge, because she looked like one of those squat bag-ladies who'd have a bird perched on her shoulder. Her outfit more or less made up of too many scarves. Then there was the wooden chopstick which impaled the grey ball of yarn, that she called hair, on top of her head.

Besides, I thought it more unbelievable that she gave Mom the thing for free!

"No. I couldn't possibly take advantage of your generosity like that!" said Mom. But who was she kidding? The only thing Mom had been worried about were the possible bedbugs going home with her.

Since an infestation a few years back, she practically runs everything through an industrial sized dryer for an hour before carting things inside. Yet still, she can't stay out of those shops.

"Oh, but I insist, Dear," said the shop keeper, "In fact I will be glad to be rid of it!"

If that wasn't a hint then I don't know what was.

"Okay," says Mom, "If you insist. But I must buy *something*. Perhaps I will get this blouse here for my daughter, Tanner."

"What a beautiful choice, Dear."

"It looks almost brand new and it's just her size!"

Another questionable finding now that I'm finally writing about it.

Mrs. Partridge took the garment and snipped the price tag from the sleeve then placed it in a brown paper bag, directing her eyes to the Square reader on the table when she saw Mom's credit card.

"Just, select there if you would like a receipt, Dear," she said.

Mom took the bag and thanked her again for her generosity. Then, she left with her paper bag in one hand and the wicker hamper under-arm.

Again, this is how it most likely happened.

And most likely, Mrs. Partridge was wringing her hands in delight.

Chapter Two

"Nan's Curiosities?"

That's what was on the bag when she handed it to me that afternoon. I can attest to that truth, as I was present.

"Just open it!" she said.

I did.

Then, when I lifted up the blouse to admire it Mom said, "It was a little shop in the Art District, and look, I got a hamper for you and Gabe's room."

Back in the Banyan

"Wait a minute!" Kristen says rolling over. She was just starting to think she'd nap her way till closing bell when Death had said it.

"You mean to say, Nan's curiosities, like the Nan's curiosities that you're standing inside of right now?"

Death turned abruptly.

He was standing beside the wooden table and had placed the old shoe there on it beside him. He glared out from under his hood which was sideways, as he was leaned over to where he could flap the lid of the hamper up and down with a narrow finger.

"Now we have the class's attention," the hollow voice said in her brain.

The skeleton flapped the lid of the old wicker hamper up and down a few times for effect. Then stood back up tall. His scythe had again joined the wooden rubbish pile.

She could tell he had been more than a little irritated at her obvious disinterest.

"I think maybe this is becoming too much for you. Perhaps we should speed things up a bit? Chronos might be ahead of schedule…"

"No. No." she said deploringly.

The rather sarcastic Grim Reaper placed his palms together in the semblance of prayer and rolled his fingertips rhythmically.

"Now, would you like I finish the story, or wouldn't you?" he asked stolidly.

She rolled back against the brick in a mix of embarrassment and relief that he hadn't decided to just give up on the whole endeavor.

The raven, just then, lit right outside of the banyan's roots in the sand and started doing that head turning thing again. She eyed it accusingly and it flew off.

Then she sighed and turned her head sideways so Death could hear her clearly and said, "Yes. Please!"

"Let's see," said the reaper. She could hear him from over her shoulder, yet under the window, verbally calculating where he had left off on the tale.

"Nan's curiosities!" she said. "Remember? She was just getting the blouse from her mom and was realizing she had bought the damn hamper here! At *this* Nan's curiosities. Geeze!"

"Oh yes," Death said.

Then as he started to recollect again, she brought her cell phone to life meaning to Google when Nan's curiosities went out of business for good, but wouldn't you know it...

No reception.

I may have been looking at the hamper mom had brought home with a bit of disgust, continued Tanner, but not because I saw anything evil about it. Actually, it had to do with the fact that I thought I'd recognized the blouse from somewhere else.

I guess that's the catch when it comes to secondhand.

"What?" Mom said sharply, "A hamper will keep your father from tripping over your clothes, if you don't fail to use it."

It was an obvious spot to insert an eyeroll. So, I did.

I followed her into my room where she cleared a small space by the bedroom door.

"There, see. It matches your dresser."

"Uh, it's great, Mom." That's when I caught a glimpse of myself in the mirror from the backside of the bedroom door. I held up the blouse.

"It's gorgeous. You should wear it to school tomorrow."

"Do you really think?" I don't always disagree with Mom. The little agreements are what kinda kept us going back then.

"Cool," said Gabe from his side of the room. He had one leg over the edge of his playpen.

He kinda coo's, really. But, when I mimic him, I always say cool, just to give him benefit of the doubt.

Mom stepped over and caught him before he fell to the floor. "No, no, Gabe. Not unless we say! You stay in your pen. No climbing!"

Just then, Dad called from the kitchen that dinner was ready.

"Well, guess he smelled the grub," I said.

"I guess so. Go wash up and I will get Gabe ready for dinner."

This is where I do the classic teenage thing and go take my shower, leaving the rest of the family waiting around the dinner table for my fashionably late arrival.

It's never intentional!

It's as I said. My dues were paid up. I was making good grades. Good choices. Plus, there's things to do in the shower.

Hair, shave, not to mention the loofa-on-a-stick is heavenly. I'm just saying, I'm not going to rush that stuff. Cleaning yourself is something you shouldn't feel forced to do quickly.

If I wanted to do that, I'd join the Navy.

Whatever. They had started without me. But, things were all-in-all okay. I missed the prayer, but it's always the same anyhow and Gabe was being fed little slivers of steak cooked medium rare. Another carnivore in the making, I guess.

I had been scrolling through Instagram when Mom said, "Tanner! Phone."

It was possibly another eyeroll moment, but Dad was watching, so I slid it under the table and onto my thigh.

"I mean it. Gabe is gonna get all your bad habits."

So, I took the hint and visibly turned off my phone, sliding it under my thigh.

We're a no-tv-at-dinner family. I mean, not all the time. But most of the time. That's okay, I get it. Dad's always at work so we like to at least eat together so he can see our faces. Would suck to work all day and not once get to enjoy what you work for.

Eew, why am I feeling sorry for military people again all of a sudden?

Anyway, dinner was great after that, actually. Then it was dishes and couch for television. Well, there's a short interlude while Mom gives Gabe some milk just to make him sleepy and the whole place is quiet. Usually, she's finished up about the time I get done doing the dishes.

Then I can kiss the little guy goodnight and Dad and I are free to turn on the tube while Mom lays down the baby.

Not really a baby anymore, but still. The baby. Classic family night, I guess.

But of course, just as I'm getting into whatever weird thing Dad has chosen on Netflix, here comes Mom. Fuming as quietly as she can over my clothes on the bedroom floor.

Must've forgot to put them in the new hamper, even though she just bought it for me. And that's what really is rubbing her wrong. Not that I didn't do it. It's that she just bought me it.

Whatever. And I would never get a chance to say this to her, but I wasn't gonna rush my washing thing. At least getting directly to the table afterward should have meant something?

Guess not.

That ended in me going to bed early. Which was fine, I'd rather swipe Instagram anyhow. Feel bad for Dad though, we don't ever get to spend time together.

I listened to the living room TV from my bed until my Dad finally came into the room. He leaned down and picked up my dirty laundry, which still was heaped defiantly in the crack of light from the opened door.

I watched as he eyed the new-to-me wicker hamper for a moment, tested its lid, which was just a simple flip up type of deal, then roll the bundle of dirtys under the lid and into the bin with a swishing sound.

He came over and sat down on the edge of the bed, putting a gentle hand on the back of my shoulder, which was intentionally facing him now.

"Ya know. We're not all that bad," he says. He gives a little pat at the statement. "You don't have to try and kill us with your dirty laundry."

Then he takes a deep breath like he's done with the humor, but maybe his dinner was just settling, "She's trying to make it easy on you. We're just asking for a little effort." Then he gently shakes my shoulders, "That's all."

Then he was probably making to kiss my head and leave it at that, but I had to say my part. And he listened. And I felt better.

Sometimes, I miss being younger. Even if I was treated like a baby.

Anyhow, I resolved to use the damned hamper after that. Another hour flipping way too much through my phone, and I was ready to pass out regardless. Water under the bridge.

The next morning, I woke up surprised to see Pixie sleeping on the lid of the antique that Gabe and I had acquired. Pixie is a Calico.

Last year, Mom would have gone ape shit had she found Pixie anywhere in the vicinity of Gabe. Something to do with cat-baby disease or something.

Recently, however, the poor thing's been allowed a little more freedom.

The danger of her falling asleep on Gabe's face and smothering him to death had seemed to pass, though Dad still liked to joke about how cats like to steal your breath at night with a kiss.

To be honest, I woke up once with a cat on my chest, not Pixie, staring right at my mouth once when I stayed at a church lock-in. Every time Dad says that it creeps me out thinking of it.

The tv was on, but no input was selected.

I rolled over and checked Gabe's crib. Nothing.

Remote on shelf? Nope.

Well, that explains that.

Just for the heck of it, and since I was already leaning over, I looked under the bed. No kid. Not that I was expecting him to be there, Mom for sure had him out in the living room for a morning slurp. But, hey, no clothes under there either.

Found the remote though.

I took the opportunity to hop up, which scared Pixie off the hamper and out of the room. Then pushed my door shut. Did my morning necessaries and changed. Nothing really to it. I've been sleeping in just a t-shirt lately, so my undies went into the hamper, which Mom had already emptied. Figures. And the tee I tossed over the bed post.

I wasn't going to disgust you with details of the whole underwear situation, but what the hell. Yes, a thong. They're comfortable.

Besides, you wear 'em while you've got the chance. Part of the month you won't be able to, what with a damn diaper hidden in your panties and all.

Too much? Yeah well, we girls wear something called bras too. Get over it.

Anyhow, I was looking forward to wearing the new blouse, but the thing smelled like moth balls so, back in the bag it went. Same old heart tee it is.

I put on my only pair of jeans that fit and made the arbitrary hall crossings to the bathroom until all was ready.

All being me.

This was Thursday morning. And not that it's your job to keep track of how many undies hit the bottom of my hamper, but that made at least one pair of panties.

Things really didn't start weirding me out till two days later, but on Friday night, I shoulda seen it coming.

Chapter Three

Between dance, and my afternoon exercise, you'd have thought that I would have at least some fresh clothes to put away on Friday night after dinner, but it just wasn't the case. Not that I would have noticed. But you kinda do that when you get accused of throwing your own clothes in the garbage.

But that wasn't the first weird thing that happened. First, the cat went missing.

Not that we would really notice Pixie missing right off the bat. Like I said, she had been on parole for a while. So, most likely, she had just been let out and not return. But no one had seen her.

That confusing situation was side railed when mom found my night shirt halfway under the bed and we got into an argument about where my panties were disappearing to.

She had said, "Well, if you'd bring me the clothes in your hamper, I would wash them for you."

I had said, in shear confusion, "What clothes?"

And that's when she scooped my shirt up off the bedroom floor and started in about the clothes I always fail to put into their proper places.

Now, you have to give me some credit here. I *had* decided to use the damn hamper. And I had been.

Okay, maybe a stray sock, or my nightgown, for God's sake, didn't make it into the antique maws of the blasted hamper, but I had been doing my duty. Now, I was in the hot seat again over some stupid clothing issue. Plus, I could tell where this ended up. Namely, with me in my room indefinitely.

I mean, if Mom and Dad wanted to spend a little time together alone, they could have just asked. But, looking back, I'm not sure they wanted to do that at all.

I could hear them out there in the living room arguing, it was embarrassing really. Who in their right mind would think I had thrown my own clothes out?

"She's doing it on purpose," then some hushes from Dad.

"Why would she do that? I had a talk with her, let's just try and calm down—"

Then Mom again, "She knows. She knows it will piss me off. I'm about to lay Gabe down and she knows it will get me upset right before his bedtime."

Then things seemed to calm down a little when they moved the argument into the kitchen.

Meanwhile, I was replacing Gabe in his crib after he had climbed out.

I always give the kid a little leeway. He had made it all the way to the dresser before I knabbed him this time.

Little escape artist.

Then, Gabe seemed pretty content, just lying in there with his blankie and his puppy dog stuffy. So, I got content too. Leaned back against my bed and started doing this connect the dots thing on my phone for a bit.

It kept me from live streaming the entire ridiculous dilemma, so, hey, give it up for patient teens. And babies.

Then I could hear Mom and Dad out there on the couch and the tv came on. One of Dad's stupid fantasy shows we watch together. Well, they're just stupid as long as you let them be. But I kinda understood what was going on.

I was just gonna let them cuddle awhile. Obviously, Mom had decided Gabe could be put down a little later, tonight. I guess sometimes, Moms need Dads too.

It had been about half of an hour. Me connecting dots, Gabe almost napping, and Mom and Dad fleetingly content when something amazing happened.

The hamper shook, nearly scaring me half to death, and Pixie's paw came over the lip of the wicker hamper, punching the lid up. Then her head popped through the top. And there she was!

"Kiki!"

Gabe was clearly excited. Seeing as that was more or less the best he'd done at naming anything but Mamma or Dadda. He was swaying there on his two feet holding the rail when she came pouring out of the hamper like nothing was amiss.

His crying out was the bedtime alarm if there ever was one. It wasn't two seconds before the tv in the living room flipped off and Mom and Dad were doing the combination tap on the door while they open it gig.

It's the parental sign of minor respect.

"Pixie," exclaimed Mom, a bit over-joyed for my blood. Usually, she'd be worried that she'd rile up Gabe, being his bedtime and all. But considering the night's events I just went with it.

"Where have you been girl?" Mom gave her all of one scratch behind the ear before Kiki, as Gabe would say, escaped to the safety of the under-bed cave.

Sure as heck beat me. I guess she'd been in the hamper all along, and that ended up being my meager response.

I was all out of eager ones. Eager was gonna have to wait till tomorrow afternoon when Mom and Dad were supposed to be going to the movies for a matinee. That was the only thing I was eager about. Gabe I can handle. House basically to myself.

Yeah, I was eager.

Dad asked if I'd like to come watch TV with them for a bit after Gabe was down, but I declined. I cranked down the brightness on my phone and lay there in my bed while Mom patted Gabe's back and got him fully to sleep. Then, I did what all good kids do at night. Give their parents space to just be.

When Mom kissed me good night and went to leave, I stopped her with a, "PSST."

I motioned for her to lift the lid on the little hamper of horrors. Then, when she did, I pulled my feet from under the quilt and stripped my socks off, turning them back right-side-out to appease her. Then, I chucked them into the basket for three points.

She shut the door with a smile.

One thing I remember above all else that night, is Pixie scaring the crap out me when she jumped up in the bed just as I was crossing over into sleep. But the one thing I remember, was her smell.

She smelled, and I know that smell now—

of old Mrs. Partridge.

The next morning, I awoke. The smell of Mrs. Partridge was quaffed by the overwhelming visual stimulation of Pixie's asshole in my face. She was stretching and folding my covers and some of my skin under-claw like dough. Not exactly a dog's morning welcome. Just saying a good licking would suffice, but hey, I guess it's nice to be kneaded.

That's an original joke by the way.

Gabe was still passed out and actually drooling. I guess he's kinda like having a dog. Maybe I did have the best of both worlds. See, sometimes I think I'm a pretty lucky girl!

It was going to be a good morning. Dad was making breakfast. I can always tell because he does the bacon in the oven first and you can't squash that smell with anything. Assholes or old ladies.

It was almost as if I had woken up in a Cinderella morning. I could envision Mom tidying the house and could actually hear Alexa playing some music in the dining room. No doubt something Christian, but the melody was good.

Just needed a couple of love birds to float out the dirty sheets onto the laundry line in the sun.

Point is, it could be a perfect morning. That fact had me moving. I wasn't gonna make the family wait for me this time, so I hopped to it before the baby awoke.

I visited the pot for a piss. No sign of the monthly uglies. Things were still looking up. I brushed my teeth and ran a brush through my hair.

If you haven't used an electric toothbrush, I would totes recommend.

They make this electric mouthpiece now I saw on Tiktok last night, where you can absolutely brush your hair while it does your teeth. Just saying. It's Twenty twenty-two.

I picked out a pair of sweats and one of my favorite striped tees cuz I was doing the whole inside-day thing today and we'll leave the unmentionables unmentioned besides saying that 'burn bra' is a thing,

I considered reusing my night shirt for tonight and after giving up on trying to smell it over the bacon, just tossed it over the bedpost again. Then the old unmentionables went into the hamper.

No mistakes this morning.

Only, the hamper was empty again. No dirty socks from last night. Had I given it more of a passing thought I may have saved myself a hell of a lot of trouble, but I swear to you, it made me stop.

Then I lifted the lid again and saw my dirty panties in there and I just kind of eyed them like they might grow feet and climb out of the hamper like Pixie did last night.

But then, Gabe was standing there looking at me like I had totally lost my mind. And it was nearly breakfast, and I was completely ready. And, it was going to be a good day.

Things were pretty uneventful up through the afternoon. Run of the mill stuff, but that is the best days if you ask me.

After breakfast, Mom started sweeping and was going to wet-mop all of the tile, which made up most of the house, so Gabe and I went out under the carport with Dad to play.

Between the swing and the chalk, Gabe has a pretty good morning, too. By the time lunch came around (it was early so that Mom and Dad could get to their date) Gabe's britches were every color of the rainbow.

I can still see the swirl of fairy dust coming from his backside as Dad brushed most of the chalk from his padded behind.

I helped Mom set up Gabe's lunch while Dad buckled him into his highchair. He had been eating these puffs that melt in his mouth lately but we had been daring to give him a bit of meat, too. So, I was breaking up a chicken nugget shaped like a brontosaurus when Dad vacated to the bedroom to get ready.

He's so cute!

Sometimes, I wish we could just let the guy throw his food all over the place, but the boy's got to learn. He seems happy though.

Mom keeps a pretty good eye on me while I feed the kid and I get it, he might choke, but ever since my trial by fire, I got this.

So, yeah. I once let Gabe stab himself with a pencil when he was one. Mom had left me with him on the floor for two seconds while I was drawing.

Before I knew it, he'd grabbed the number two with no eraser left and jabbed himself right in the chubby little thigh.

There's still a little blue dot there where the lead went in. Dad called poison control and everything. Luckily, pencil lead isn't real lead, it's graphite so it's non-toxic.

But still, every time I play with his cute chubby thighs I'm reminded about letting him get my pencil. It was traumatic.

Still, I don't know what was worse, Gabe's wailing, or Mom's.

Anyhow, the boy and I are fine on our own. While he finished eating, I nibbled on dinosaurs as Mom explained the essentials. Puffs? Check. Diapers? Check. Bouncy chair? Ready. Milk?

Nah, she'd be back before dinner.

But even if she wasn't, I was more than confident that I could get along with Gabe. I mean, we were siblings and all. Besides, Dad has a camera in the living room so he can see what's up at any moment.

I don't think it is an intruder thing.

I think he just likes to be able to see us enjoying what he's working for while he's gone on business trips. He's tried to scare us a few times by remotely connecting to it and pretending to be an otherworldly presence through its speaker. Flickering the blue tooth lighting was a nice touch, but it was still just cheesy. So, maybe it's just a toy.

Mom had everything set up as set-up could be before her and Dad were walking out the door. Gabe was gonna be napping most of the time they were out anyhow. I just couldn't let him sleep too long or he'd be hard to put down tonight. And I was not gonna have a bad end to my perfect day.

So, I assured them both they were leaving the place in good hands, hugged them, and then held my breath as they backed out of the drive.

Chapter Four

Dim the lights, turn down the air, grab a quilt, and dive into the corner pocket of the couch. Snuggled behind the ever-present glow of the I-phone. All mine. You'd be surprised how dark it gets in here with the blackout curtains pulled.

Sometimes, when I'm home alone like this, I ask myself, "Is this what life is supposed to be like?"

I'm nearly convinced that it is.

Though, Mom would have me believe that life is out there in the church somewhere.

Dad would have me think that life is out there in the woods, or at work… who knows. But for me, I could do this right here forever.

Gabe is in there sleeping. I'm safe. I can actually watch Grey's Anatomy and enjoy it. I can stop it halfway through and switch to Glee. If I want company, any number of peeps are on Facebook messenger; a videochat away.

It's hard to even think of this house being stressful while alone in here with Gabe. I mean, what is the literal problem most of the time?

This is easy.

I was sitting there, in the relative silence, since I had seen that episode of Grey's before, the volume was down and I was thinking of what next to type into the little messenger window to Kelly.

So far, it had just been our complaining about family life and how marriage is the last thing on the planet we'd be interested in. But, when I was considering the good company of pets, I realized I hadn't seen Pixie all day.

When the thought struck, a strange sound came from the bedroom. And I stopped cold.

Something was chewing.

Okay. So, something is chewing on something in the baby's room AKA my bedroom.

I'm not one to read horror novels. But I've seen my share of scary movies; at least parts of them. While rationality holds a high seat in a household prone to practical jokes, I still hadn't dismissed the idea of a panty thief after yesterday's charades.

Okay, something in there eating my panties is a gross thought, but hey, I'm a girl, alone, and the last episode of Glee sported some high school guys inadvertently spreading chlamydia through the sharing of a pocket pussy. So, sue me.

So, I did what any semi-rational teenager, home alone would do in that instance. I opened up Instagram and started recording.

The distance from the couch to the bedroom door is approximately twenty feet. But I had to make my way around the coffee table and past a bookshelf to get to it. Every step I kept thinking that the sound would go away. That maybe it was just something from the tv which was mounted by the bookshelf.

Sound has the tendency to bounce in this big, tiled space.

But every tile I covered with my socked feet, quilt wrapped around me, it just kept coming.

Munch. Smack. Munch.

By the time I passed the bookshelf I was raising Instagram up for a good look at the bedroom door, and probably looked like the emperor from Star Wars, but I wasn't flipping the camera for whatever viewers to see me in my day-at-home attire.

However, I did make the commentary, "Do you hear that?"

A fact I wouldn't realize until later. It just kinda came out when I was talking to myself. Another bad habit, I guess.

When I was reaching for the door handle, I had pretty much decided that the chewing was definitely coming from the vicinity of the hamper. In fact, I knew it was!

I stopped, picturing all kinds of horrific things a hamper might look like if it came to life. Everything from some stupid book I saw in the Evil Dead to a wicker doll of some sort with a panty fetish. I was gonna chicken out and wait until the chewing stopped.

It had to stop eventually, right?

But then I realized, Gabe was in there!

That gave me strength. Not because I am some super-protective hero who would throw herself in harm's way for the baby.

I would, if it came down to that. But, it was because, there was a damn baby in there sleeping. Or maybe awake! And if he wasn't freaking out, then why should I?

Was a man, or a girl, or whatever? Or was I a mouse?

Still, I didn't want to wake Gabe if I could help it.

I cracked the door enough to see Gabe snoozing in the crib.

The chewing abruptly stopped.

I think that scared me more than anything else. So, I did the smart thing and sacrificed the viewers like a lamb to slaughter. I poked my phone through the crack of the door where the camera would get a good shot of the deadly hamper.

The chewing started again, and I was positive that I had just gotten a peek at an inanimate object devouring a pair of dirty underwear on my Insta! So, I pushed the door open in a blaze of brainless glory; feeling a lot like Mom trying to scold me through whispers.

It was that point in my life, that I sided fully with my father and decided that I did not like cats!

Pixie was going to town on a dinosaur nugget which she had become extremely protective over and she was gnawing it ragged on top of that damn flimsy hamper lid.

When she caught sight of the glowing emperor from Star Wars closing in on her she bolted for under the bed. Her claws caught the wicker of the hamper, which weighed next to nothing with only under garments in it, and the thing came tumbling down on its side toward Gabe's crib.

I instinctively tried to catch it when my feet went right out from under me in a mix of quilt and socks on the tile threshold.

The Insta viewers would have a spiraling view of my bedroom until the phone hit the carpeted floor.

All of it happened in a second. And besides the handle of the bedroom door protesting under my weight as I tried to catch myself, the debacle was relatively silently executed. Well, followed by my laughter, that is. The laughing at the end is probably what later got it featured as one of those 'Oh, no' out takes on Tiktok.

Yeah. It was going to be a winner. Truth be told, when I realized I was still rolling, I sold it with a little extra laughter while lying there on my back. But the greatest thing was, It didn't wake the baby.

Or so I had thought.

I rolled over onto my knees and reached like a cat (I now hate cats).

The phone was just inside the door on the floor by the overturned hamper. In reach enough not to further disturb Gabe's nap.

When I eased the door shut, I turned the phone to a face shot and said, "Well, that didn't go as planned."

Tapped stop on the screen.

Then, I scrambled to my feet and did a sock slide across the tile floor to the couch that would have made Tom Cruise jealous. Piled back into the bundle of the couch corner. And all was well.

The dumbest thing about all of this is that if I wouldn't have actually watched my video before uploading it, like Mom taught me, I may have never known that the hamper was haunted.

I was literally laughing about the whole thing with Kelly on Facetime while we were watching the Instagram video when she made the comment that set it all off.

"At least it wasn't a panty thief!" Kelly said.

That was as I was re-watching it and trying to get the creepy music, I was sticking to it to sync-up.

It was frozen during the upload at the exact moment when Pixie had leapt off of the Hamper, turning it over. My phone got great footage of the whole thing. But, before the phone went tits up on the floor by the bed, I noticed something that disturbed the shit out of me.

In that frozen shot I could clearly see that the hamper was empty.

I sat bolt upright on the couch.

My socks! I had thrown my socks in the hamper last night for three points. There would at least be socks!

Okay, unless Mom washed a load this morning. But I was sure I hadn't heard the dryer running today.

I went to the washer and dryer; our units are just stuffed into a nook off the kitchen. The lid on the washer was open. A moist washcloth was draped over the head of the agitator, otherwise empty.

No neat piles of clothes on top of the dryer.

I grabbed the thick plastic of the dryer handle and pulled. It's always such a reinforced effort when I open the dryer, like a magnet is fighting against my pull.

The clasp finally released with a bang.

Nothing but lint.

Hair curled up at the nape of my neck.

Mom would never have washed just a pair of socks, and even if she did, what happened? Had they gone off and joined the fuckin' puppet show?

That's when I heard Gabe cry. Instantly, I remembered him stabbing himself with that pencil by mistake.

But this was no accident.

If I try and tell you what I was feeling in that horrible moment, it will fall short.

I've heard people on Youtube talk of their near-death experiences, you know, when they say life flashes before their eyes and all that. Well, that's the kind of weird stuff that I felt in that moment.

Like, everything happens at once, and there is time for that, which is impossible, but there was.

In one second, I knew that damned hamper was wicked. In that same second, I was sliding around the corner of the kitchen toward the bedroom. Then Pixie was crying like she was in heat. But it sounded like the cry was coming from inside of a cave.

And I knew. I just KNEW that the cat was inside the gaping maw of that horrible hamper, crying out for Gabe or crying out in angst against whatever evil had come from that terrifying void and swallowed him up.

A bright light was shining from the cracks along the doorway. It was an orange that reminded me of the inside of a desert cave, or an Egyptian temple at dawn. And when I pushed into the room, a great starburst of light filled my vision from where the curtains to outside had been drawn back.

The lock was still bolted.

There was the wicker dresser. White and blue. The overturned hamper that matched. My daybed against the wall, perfectly made, besides a small cyclone of disturbed fabric where the cat may have made up roost.

Had I imagined the sounds?

No. Gabe's crib was empty.

The wicker hamper was on its side with the lid opened like an inviting spot to hide in a game of hide-n-seek. It too was empty.

And the room was blanketed in abject silence.

My breath caught as I realized that what I was looking at was probably the most horrifying thing I had ever seen in my life. It may have been my bedroom, but there was no life in there. No baby breathing nor drooling. Nor cooing.

Just a scene that suggested the impossible.

To my horror, a trail of blue and pink chalk led from the crib to the hamper.

Gabe and probably Pixie, had gone into the hamper and now were gone.

Chapter Five

Now, I know teens are notorious for doing drugs. Not me, okay. But this was something that happened to kids who ate mushrooms or dabbed on those pens, or whatever the hell.

There I was, alone in my room. It might be hard to imagine what I was going through, so let me help you.

My Dad once told me on the basketball court when I asked him about what he believed in, he said,

"Ya know. I can't really tell you that. All I know is, one day I felt myself grow like, I realized that if I kept zooming out from my pupil, I would eventually see myself again if I ever escaped the confines of the Universe. But I've read a lot of fiction."

He had looked at me with kinda a thoughtful eye. And then, seeing I had been looking for real guidance, he said, "Proof is found in truths you experience for yourself."

Well, that is what I felt in that instance. Like the whole world just got really solid, really fast. I had experienced something. And now, suddenly nothing mattered but my choices in this room, this house.

Right then, everything was still private, well, besides my Insta video which would soon go viral. But I had a choice to make.

Call the police? Call my parents?

What if they called me crazy? What if I was crazy! What if I was stark raving mad?

Slowly, I backed out of the bedroom and into the living room. My body was tingling all over. I realized I hadn't taken a breath in forever and finally gasped. I was going to hyperventilate and have a panic attack.

Before I knew it, I was sitting on the couch with my hands on my knees and taking huge rasping breaths in the sound of Gabe. Gabe. Gabe.

Then, I thought of what might happen if someone found out what was going on before I figured this all out.

I was gonna lose it. I looked at the front door as if I might just run outside into the light and escape back to reality and that's when I saw the nanny cam mounted over the door.

Oh shit! I thought. Dad may be watching me this instant. What if he sees me freaking out?

Get yourself together Tanner. Just breathe. You can do this. Just go back there and see what's what. Then, slowly, I managed to stop shaking enough. Conscious of the camera, I took my feet, forced a smile and made my best casual exit stage right. I even did a pirouette.

I know, dumb.

As soon as I was in the hall I fell in a heap against the wall by the opened bedroom door and sucked air, hard. I was gonna vomit. The bathroom door was open so I made for the sink.

My own reflection got me focused again and I gripped the side of the vanity forcing myself to look in the mirror.

"You're okay!" I said, twisting the cold-water knob.

I grabbed a handful of water and splashed my face with it. Then I turned and howled, as if I had just woken from a dream while sleep walking, "Gabe?"

Nothing. I stumbled back to Mom and Dad's room and pretended I was groggy. Physically acting like I was just dreaming while looking around for a sign of him or Pixie.

"Gabe!" I screamed in desperation.

I was in my parent's bathroom now and knew I was only fooling myself. The sound of my scream was still echoing in my ears.

I wasn't dreaming. This was happening, and if I kept this up, the neighbors were going to call the police.

I put my face in my dad's towel. Then, when I came up for air, I intentionally walked directly back to my bedroom and took a good look around.

There was no denying it.

The chalk told the whole story. Little Gabe footprints in pink and blue across the carpet. Little Gabe handprints on the inside cotton flap of that damned hamper.

A once, cushioned-butt baby boy, smiling in the chalk-play under the carport was lost. Gone to wherever that hamper had taken him.

What was I saying?!

A hamper ate my brother and cat?

I dropped to my hands and knees and stared into the cotton lining of the thing, imaging my brother crawling inside.

Is that really what had happened? He just crawled right in?

I looked desperately under the bed in total denial and in one last effort to see reason. He had to be hiding! But it was unreasonable as me trying to act like I was sleep walking.

I reached an arm out toward the mouth of the open hamper, then I retracted it.

If I went to sleep in a dream would I wake up back in the real world? It was worth trying. I put my hands on the bed thinking to pull myself up and get under the covers and then I thought,

"Who am I kidding? I'm not gonna sleep for weeks." I pulled at the hair on the top of my head until it hurt in frustration.

Then I remembered something I had seen in one of Kelly's cultish Hexcraft books.

Mom would have spit nails if she'd ever found out Kelly was into all that stuff.

It had been an entry that had suggested that if you ever found yourself trapped in the otherworld, just put your thumb in your mouth and bite down hard. I did, really hard. More from anger than anything.

I was most definitely in the real world, even if what was happening was unrealistic. And now my thumb was throbbing under the nail.

I suddenly felt like life was unreasonably unfair. It would figure that the one chance this week I get time to be myself I would be stuck doing this. I almost wanted to kick the hamper and fall down in a heap crying.

"This is bullshit!" I spit out just under my breath.

I told you somethings would be loads of crap. I hope you agree by now.

Then, I actually spat. Spat right at the wall behind the hamper where I had hung my fucking baptism certificate. It was defiant and almost scared me that I could be so angry.

But I felt a little better.

All of a sudden, I didn't really care what was going to happen. I just wanted to do it, and quite frankly get back to my god damned Grey's.

Well, I'd seen what's what.

Kids I tell you. You give them an inch of leeway and they take a mile.

I looked down into the tiny cloth cave. Okay, eyeroll definitely justified.

Fuck it. I guess I'm going in there.

Chapter Six

The first thing you think of when you are shoulders deep inside of a dirty clothes hamper, well, besides I'm nuts, is the real possibility of developing pink eye.

I had initially tested the waters by reaching my hand to the bottom, of course. Nothing strange there. I watched my fingers crawl across the fabric. It was the bottom of a cloth bag, and I could feel the coarse wicker wood beneath it.

I pulled my arm out and turned the basket right-side-up. The lid fell closed when I did, with a slap! I'd be lying if I said I didn't flinch, like I was about to get punched in the face by the thing.

Then, I slowly folded the top back again, half expecting to see my little brother screaming up from the mouth of some hellish hole in the bottom of the thing, half expecting Pixie to jump out and scare me shitless, and half-hoping that anything else would happen.

I couldn't decide if nothing happening would be better or worse than something hellish. So, I didn't look at all when I opened it. I just folded back the lid and reached in again all the way up to the shoulder.

While the hamper had been lying on the floor, I had easily reached the bottom of the basket. My arm was a good hand and a half longer than the hamper was tall or deep.

But now, my arm was buried to the shoulder.

I opened my eyes, intentionally averting my gaze above my bed, and my hand was still… hovering, in whatever space there was below where there should be cloth and wood.

In that moment, I realized I was looking directly at my dreamcatcher, spinning there, and it made me consider all of the strange movies I had seen where the fabric of reality wasn't all that tangible after all.

With the thought, I started to consider looking into where my hand was reaching down into some other intangible place and when I did, my hand felt as if it were no longer just floating in empty space but being enshrouded by something.

That feeling coupled by the thought that my brother may have been eaten, scared me dead numb.

Momentarily I was frozen with fear, thinking I may look in and see my hand in the throat of the hamper, complete with teeth and eyes and— if I saw that, I was going to die. It wouldn't have to eat me; I was going to outright die of something more terrible.

It would have literally scared me to fucking death.

Hell, just the thought of it nearly did that.

It paralyzed me. I will tell you that.

I couldn't look. I mean, I couldn't look and keep my hand in there. It was simply instinctive now to get my hand back from wherever it was as quickly as possible.

But, before I jerked my hand free and turned my head to look, I grabbed whatever the hell it was enshrouding my fingers and hand, then I yanked my arm out so fast that you'd think I had found my arm in boiling water.

As I stood up with a jerk, I saw whatever horrible thing I had yanked out of that other place and screamed, dropping it like it had been a branding iron I'd grabbed.

I shouldn't have to tell you how you'd feel when you've unexpectedly pulled a red deflated thing, the exact size and shape of a baby through from possibly another world.

I was terrified!

I knew exactly why they called them Goosebumps, because I felt like a plucked and naked goose at that instant in my existence. Cold little pimples all over.

But, then I felt duped.

Hanging there, half in and half out of the hamper from hell, was a child's onesie. Not one I had ever seen Gabe wear, either.

The lid had closed on it when I dropped the thing in horror.

The red thing I had pulled, like a rabbit out of a magician's hat, was a piece of clothing!

Well, that would make sense from a hamper! But this was no magic act. At least not one that I was finding entertaining.

I was still not eager to touch the thing again, but reluctantly, and after many deep breaths to calm myself down and then again, some gentle self-coaching, I assured myself that I wasn't just a batshit fucking lunatic.

Then, I grabbed it. First with two fingers, and then lifted the lid and drew it fully out, holding it up.

It was a fucking onesie alright.

And it still had the price tag on it.

I threw back the lid. Nothing there.

I looked at the onesie with disgust.

The price tag didn't have a JCPenny logo on it or anything like that. It was just a handwritten four ninety-nine, without a bother to even jot a dollar symbol.

You don't get a red cotton onesie, especially one with the bunny ears-hoodie, for four ninety-nine just anywhere.

I picked up the hamper. Turned it upside down and shook it. Dust motes floated down defiantly. I looked up at it, then closed my eyes and held it aloft shaking it some more.

Gabe nor Pixie fell to the floor.

I put the damned thing on like a hat. And this is where I left off talking about pinkeye.

There was no way in hell I was going to pass through this hamper with my shoulders, not to mention my hips, but we won't go there.

The hair on my head scarcely brushed the bottom of the thing because it tapers as it goes down. The hamper, not my head.

It was a yellow sanctum in there for a moment. In front of my face was Gabe's little blue handprint, and I thought of being inside of an Indian teepee.

I looked down at my feet and saw the red onesie hanging in my left hand. Then, I shut my eyes and took a breath. For a moment, I felt as if the atmosphere had changed. It was warmer, though it could have been my breath. But it smelled.

Shut up.

It smelled like moth balls.

When I opened my eyes, I was still in my bedroom. The smell was gone, and I removed the hamper from my head, dropping it in its proper place.

Slowly I lifted the red onesie to my nose and sniffed. Moth balls!

There was something else in my bedroom that had smelled like that. Was it possible Mom was getting over her fear of bedbugs? She must have been in a rush and skipped running it through the dryer. And, that had been the reason I hadn't worn it the day after Mom had brought it home.

I went to my closet and pulled open the accordion doors. Up there on the shelf, was my blouse. It hadn't had a price tag on it to compare. But it was still in the bag.

The bag that read, Nan's Curiosities.

A quick search on Google Maps pulled up the little shop. It was in the Art District all right. Less than two miles from the house. But it wouldn't be a cheery jaunt to get there.

That was the thing about this town. My dad had called our place a diamond in the rough because it was across from the elementary school. Under the umbrella and relative safety of the parking lot's streetlamps, and no doubt, a bit more city funding.

But, if you pedal your bike two blocks in either direction, you'd quickly realize that your existence is an island in the ghetto.

No matter. There's a number listed.

I'll just politely call them and tell them I have one of their clothing items that I would like to exchange for my little brother and my cat, and as a matter of fact they can take back this god damned hamper, before I shove it down their god damned throat!

Sorry.

And... there's a busy signal. Not a busy signal like the one you hang up and call back later. The busy signal that says you've reached the end of the line and have never been told what this shorter, more rapid, boop boop boop noise is supposed to mean, busy signal.

I grabbed the bag with the blouse, thinking I would need some excuse (besides crazy) to be at the shop, and thought about putting on my shoes.

But then I caught a glimpse of myself in the door mirror and decided it would be against better judgement to bike through the ghetto without a bra on.

What I needed was a ninja suit. This was a mission.

My inner voice became my mother as I gently reminded myself that I wasn't going on a bike ride through the ghetto. I was going on a short trip to the Art District.

I felt like I was breaking out of jail or something.

First off; the furthest I've ever wandered from home, besides the bus stop, has been on Halloween, and that's with my parents.

Okay, I admit, that sounds a little lame. But I told you, I'm a good kid!

Next; Dad had that stupid camera over the living room door to the outside, so it wasn't going to make for an easy exit.

I can't climb out of my bedroom window because our next-door neighbor is the king of snoop. Besides, threatening to shoot us if we play in his yard, if he saw me and tried to talk to me, I would likely have to fake a medical emergency just to end the conversation. At least that's what Mom says she has to do.

He's the kind of person who gets so deep into the 'well, when I was younger' and then follows it up with a ' like I said', ad infinitum.

Start talking to him and my parents would be pulling in the drive before I ever got a start on the bike.

That leads me to the last issue. Time.

I believe I can get down to the shop and back in half an hour. It's been at least that since Gabe's disappearance and movies only last so long.

I'm thinking I might have an hour on the safe side to be back here with my brother.

But let's be realistic here. Okay, that's laughable. In reality, if such a place as Reality still exists, I'd just like some answers between now and when either the cops get me, or my parents show up and have me committed.

I went out my parent's window.

I'd seen Dad pop that screen off enough times to plug the electric weed-eater in while he cut the backyard. You'd think he was a racist if you'd ever been subject to him using that thing.

I mean, weed eaters probably don't have feelings, but c'mon we have neighbors.

Anyhow, the screen popped right out. Besides the curtain rod falling off its cheap little metal tabs and ending up on my head during my escape, I'd say it went pretty well. Other than the ruler shaped bruise which I would likely be sporting; right across my stomach.

The bruise, no one will notice because I'm wearing a onesie of my own. Specifically, a unicorn one I had worn last Halloween. Don't laugh.

Thanks to my hamper eating my only pair of jeans that fit, the onesie seemed to be the most convenient thing to put on (after a bra), and it actually goes pretty good with sneakers.

It has a hood!

As a teenage girl who is about to be trucking it through the ghetto slash Art District, I'm gonna feel safer with my hood up. The less skin showing, the better. No weirdos are gonna be perving on a chick in a onesie with a unicorn horn.

For real though, I still wasn't over being comfortable today.

Besides, I was on a mission. But it was a mission to save a baby.

So, it wasn't a ninja suit, but what could be less threatening to Gabe than his sister in the unicorn onesie they trick-or-treated in together?

Escape? Check. Bike? Check. Bag from Nan's little shop of horrors? Check.

I even had a sparkly cloth mask from back when Covid was bad. As I pedaled away from my island in the ghetto and toward the Art District I thought, I might be the hero in this little story.

It definitely wasn't the guy on the corner of Nineteenth and Tamiami, who was hiding from the sun under the dried-up fronds of a couple malnourished palm trees.

Those were unfortunate souls. Just as the palms themselves were unfortunate to have been inhabiting the parking lot of this blocks most recently failed business.

Rugged individuals drinking beer from paper bags. Sidewalks cracked beneath the heat of the Florida sun. A flyer for the Lumpin Family Circus got pasted against the spokes of my front tire while I waited at a stop sign and I remembered how it was back before little brothers.

It all passed behind me when I crossed the main intersection. Probably they saw me a lot like my dad saw our house. A unicorn, riding her nice bicycle through an urban desert.

A diamond in the rough.

In truth, I couldn't care what they thought. It was supposed to be my day and I was going to be comfortable!

Chapter Seven

The Art District was a little different during the day, from how it had been at night on Halloween. Like, I remembered walking through here, but I wouldn't have known what I was looking at.

A cute wooden sign sported a parrot with three different arrows, indicating three different directions, obviously. One was green and simply labeled ARTIST. It pointed along the road to my left, where the sidewalk was painted in different colors becoming a game of hopscotch. Another was painted blue and said GEM MINE. That one's sidewalk became a rougher cobble type of stones off to the right. Between the stones looked like water ran through them, but it was noticeably an artificial design. The one pointing in the direction that I knew I was going was painted red. On it, was written NAN's.

There was no sidewalk going straight ahead like there were going to each side, but I could see the loping ropes that marked off the shelly parking area before the shop.

A bunch of beachy decorations were on this side of the building. It was landscaped with palmettos and palms, interspersed with an occasional conch, or life saver buried in the sand and shells. A miniature wooden windmill stood crookedly in the garden. If you could call it a garden. A rock garden of bleached and crushed shells, maybe.

While I crossed the road, I'd heard the sound of a water wheel running off to my right, from where the sign had pointed to the GEM MINE. My curiosity peaked, but I knew I was short on time.

Approaching the front of Nan's was kinda like walking up to the front of a giant crab that had lifted its head from the sand.

The front door of the shop was set back under the shadow of the crab's brow. Pilons, big wooden posts, stretched out and to the sides from the bottom of the steps that lead up there. An ancient rope drooped along the pilons, marking the lot, and making it look like the place had claws buried in the sand on each side.

To the left and right of the entrance were adobe railings and these glistened with candle holders of different shapes and sizes. Then, out in the sandy alcoves were wooden trees, though I guess ladders might be a better way of describing them, that were strung with all sorts of beads and headdresses.

There was a reflective and color-changing ball sitting in a small marble fountain off to the right as I approached, and the courtesy pelican, but none of it took away from the overall feeling of walking into the great face of a giant crab.

I could have lost my bike against the adobe wall, right there beneath those Mardi Gras beads, it was just like adding another piece to a sculpture. But I left it there, where I thought it would be reasonably safe.

Then I walked up the five shallow steps, right under, what seemed to me, the eyebrows of the great crab and into the shadow of the entrance.

It was cooler there, out of the sun. The vinyl sign stuck to the glass above the door wasn't recent. It spelled out the name of a shop which had been a staple. This was a shop that had dug its roots in long ago. It was the biggest and it was the one that looked least like a house and more like an animal that belonged.

Nan's Curiosities.

The bell over the door jingled as I stepped into the musty shop. It jingled again when I eased the door back closed, and the top edge hit the little rocker making the tail of a little iron gargoyle.

I know. Classic horror-shop bullshit. But if you're not warmed up by now on the unbelievable then there's not much else I can do to prepare you for what happens next.

I was there, in that shop.

A stuffed crow arched over the doorway from its petrified perch gawking at the long yellow skull of some creature; maybe a horse. The entrance hall was close quarters beneath that.

Most of whatever she had stacked up alongside the doorway was covered in black lacey material.

I could see a glass case in the far recess of the shop, out beyond where the little punk rock-themed welcome area opened up. As I paced forward, I got more an eye of the place and knew more certainly that somehow this particular place in the spacetime continuum connected to that hamper back at home.

How? Well, I will tell you.

The smell.

Gabe was here somewhere.

I was sure of it.

Chapter Eight

I took the hood from the uni-onesie down off my slightly sweaty head and stepped confidently out into the main room of the shop.

In front of me was the glass case, housing a variety of jewelry. Rings, some with giant green gemstones. Necklaces with diamonds of different cuts, maybe quartz. The rings may have been emerald I might guess. Fake or not, who knew.

I also saw other things in the case that didn't seem so precious. An old tape-recorder, silverware, what I hoped was a rubber snake swallowing its own tail, and shark teeth. Admittedly some were as large as my hand, but I still couldn't see why they'd be locked away.

The combination sales counter and jewelry case didn't keep my attention long. Behind the counter was an archway leading to a room in the back and I could hear the tenant back there moving things around. Maybe sliding cardboard boxes.

The archway was made into a privacy door via beads and little plastic bones hanging on strings. It was thickly woven and hung there motionless.

"Be out in a moment!" came her voice for the first time. Then, "Have a look around!"

I did, and noticed a camera up in the corner by the door I had entered through.

Otherwise, there were archways much like the one behind the counter leading off to my left and right. Through the archway on the right looked like where the secondhand clothing was.

I could see the round silver racks packed thick with garments on hangers.

The room beyond the archway on the left looked a little more mysterious, or its contents anyway. There was smoke from an incense stick twirling up in there, and a multicolor lightshow was spinning, as I could see the colors on the wall moving.

But, before investigating further, I reached down into the woven basket by the counter and removed one of the long colorful bamboo sticks. It was as think as my arm at least and sealed on both ends.

I know what you're thinking and no, I wasn't going to clobber anyone with it. Actually, at that point I was feeling relatively safe being in the quaint, if not creepy, little shop rather than out on the streets.

I was just curious.

It's kinda funny telling this story, because I realize I've said things like, Nan's shop of horrors and the cursed hamper. But, at the time, I was just a kid doing what came naturally.

I don't know what this would have come out like if I had told it the week after it happened. Probably not so much cussing. But, then again, maybe so.

I was pretty brave after all. Still might have been worried about getting an ass whopping if my parents read it.

But, nowadays I've read half the stuff my dad has written and he's no angel. In fact, he said when you're writing, and shit is what you mean to say. Say shit. Don't say phooey.

Makes sense, I guess. Someone who says fiddlesticks probably isn't sneaking out their parent's bedroom window.

Now that I've cleared that up, I was looking at this bamboo thing and the hour glass symbol that had been painted on its side.

So I turned it over, naturally.

Then came the sound of a rainstorm. It must've had a billion beads inside of it to make that sound. I was listening to all of them pinging off of the channels inside the bamboo as they descended. Getting louder every second.

PHHHSSSSHSHHHH.

When out of nowhere, she was standing there behind the counter. Those teeth I would not yet know how to explain, hidden so perfectly under her puffy top lip and above the stone chin.

There was an immediate desire to look her directly in the eye because to look at her mouth was both disgusting and embarrassing. A mole was on her chin that had two hairs sticking out of it as thick as fishing line.

But when I moved my eyes to hers and saw that one pupil was drowned under a film of white gloss, my attention found nowhere to land and I was thrown completely off my high horse where I had been ready to do battle.

Now, I couldn't even find a way to look at this short old woman without offending her, much less address her.

The makeshift rainstorm must have covered the sound of the beads when she came through. Now, the rain staff was clattering to the floor.

"I'm sorry," I said, trying to grab it before it rolled under the lip of the counter. When I came back up I had to push my damn unicorn horn back from my face again and that's when I really got a good look at her.

She reached out across the glass and took the staff, assisting me as we both returned it to the basket on my side of the counter.

It was a long arm for such a short thing and the skin that was revealed on the forearm was more of an ashen color of green.

"It's okay, Dear," she said, and now I felt like Pixie must have felt when I caught her with that dino nugget, because I was the one looking at the emperor from Star Wars. Except this one didn't have a hood. And it was a She. Determined only by the excess of hair atop her head and, well, the excess bosom atop the counter.

The rain stick made a hollow sound when it was set back against its neighbors again and I suppressed the overwhelming urge to apologize once more.

Instead, I opted for something less conspicuous.

"That's pretty cool," I said. And it was true, too. Even better.

There was a strange silence before she answered, and in it I thought she was trying to determine if I was up to no good. A sane kid would have turned tail and run.

I mean she looked like a beagle (a dog detective) with her cloudy eye surveying me and one of her bottom incisors stuck outside of her upper lip.

But I was a unicorn. Not any old kid. So, I just put it down and acted innocent.

"What is it?" I asked.

"Storm stick," she barked. That eye just glaring.

Then, I was totally flustered and wasn't entirely sure how I was going to buy time to look around without causing suspicion, so I pretended I was... well...

a dimwit.

I picked up the storm stick, which was the last thing she'd have expected, and shook it like a shake weight, or a saltshaker. Or a tambourine, whatever you prefer. Point is, I shook the thing, and she hadn't been fast enough to stop me from grabbing it again.

But I let her snatch it from me a moment later and stuff it harshly back in its basket. I assumed the look of a downtrodden toddler.

"Do that too much and you'll make it rain I tell you!" she seethed.

"Really?" I asked overly interested.

That eye was getting fishy again. But I didn't give her time to consider my act.

"What's that?" I asked. Pointing to the shiniest red ruby under the glass. My eyes wide as I could make them.

"Well, that's the red ruby of Mars," Mrs. Partridge began gently explaining, "mined from the Mountains of Snowdownia."

I drifted over it like her words were a tractor beam. She was buying my act.

"They say if you let the moonlight shine through it, you can instantly create a flame!" The crone's hands did a little finger dance in the air.

I followed her fingers. "Wooooow!"

For a second I thought she might do a magic trick, but I wanted to finish my own act.

"And what's this?" I said quickly, bending the tip of my finger over the old-fashioned tape recorder under the glass.

Her good eye found me, this time with some surprise and she said stolidly, "That's... a tape player."

I looked up at her as innocently as I could muster, "Ahhhhh."

She was looking at me with both eyes now, though I wasn't sure how well either of them worked, when I pretended to have interest in a particularly dainty golden scale that was precariously balanced with intricate little weights. I shot a hand toward it a bit recklessly and said, "and this?"

She fell for my feint and the gnarled little hand that had been performing for me a moment ago began to reach up in an attempt to ward of my reckless excitement but drew back when she decided I exercised at least *some* control.

I couldn't tell if there was any worry in her eyes because they didn't change. But her movement seemed to tell me that I had her right where I wanted.

"To measure the herbs," she said cautiously eyeing the box of tied cloth baggies off to the right.

Then as quickly as it was out of her mouth, I put my hands down directly on the array of wooden piccolos laid out on the counter. I began sliding three separate ones back and forth like I were deciding which one I wanted to put in my mouth and test.

Instantly her hand fell on top of the simple woodwind instruments, pinning them down.

"Instruments," she stated coldly.

Then, I delivered the final blow. My left hand went quickly to the dream catcher that was hanging on my left. It was much nicer than mine but just as fragile.

At that point, I knew she might have an idea that I could be a little special, but I wasn't stupid. I wasn't going to destroy the dreamcatcher. Also, I didn't want the poor woman hurting herself trying to save the darn thing from my witless wrath.

So, I stood up much taller than she and quickly plucked it off of its nail by the string. There seemed to be nothing more threatening than an agile invalid.

And, that seemed to do it.

With a great exasperated sigh of relief, Mrs. Partridge came round the edge of the counter and gingerly lifted the Dreamcatcher down from my incompetent grip and placed it on the counter.

"This, is a dream catcher, Dear. Now," and I could see her working out that her involvement here was only making things worse, "look around if you'd like, but, please! Don't touch anything!"

I nodded a little, with hands up pretending to examine the thing as she retreated.

"I'll just be moving some things in the back. Call if you need some assistance."

Then, as she passed through the beads, I imagined that a whole nother store may be back there beyond that veil.

I could worry about that later.

First, I had to look around.

I meandered through the part of the shop that was hiding out under the archway on my left. There were tons of antiques and oddities that I will spare you most of, only because that was leading me nowhere.

But, there were cool things I would have loved to have for my own. I would have come back and purchased that salt rock lamp, I mean, if my brother was okay, of course.

It wasn't until I was over on the other side of the shop and circling the clothes racks that I found something mentionable. Mom says, if something is mentionable then it's manageable, but this was not going to be manageable.

I was sliding the clothes hangers, more or less one by one, and trying not to be disgusted by the fact that overalls, dresses, and infant shorts were all racked together, when I saw my jeans.

Definitely mine. I pulled the legs out to assess them while they were still attached to the roundy thingy. The legs, light blue faded at the knees with little tears that looked cosmetic but could only have been created by yours truly's, designed-by-use. I looked in the waistband.

Embarrassingly, this is how I knew for certain. Even though I knew by the look of them, but they had those little elastic bands with buttons inside that made them fit my hips perfect. I looked sideways through the archway back at the register as if the little old thief might be standing there and see my reaction, and a sound may not have escaped me, giving away my surprise if I hadn't seen the price tag.

A dollar!?

"Huh!" I squealed.

A buck? She was selling my one and only pair of jeans for a buck? I had removed the jeans from the hanger and was holding them out to the camera (now I had noticed that there was one in every room). I just couldn't help myself.

"Really?" I said to it, defiantly.

This time I could hear the beads make their swishes and swooshes when she came through.

So she had been watching me on a screen back there. Or had she only heard my remark?

She approached the counter and enveloped it again with her bosom. She was silent, thus far and that chin of hers reminded me of a toad. I half expected her to knab a fly if I asked her where she had gotten the pants, but I thought that fact was apparent. The price tag was the same kind of tag that was on that red onesie I had pulled through on the other side.

And the writing. Exact same. No money sign, just a lazy scribble.

I took the pants to the counter. I told the old heifer, "I just threw these pants in the hamper yesterday morning! Now, they are on your rack."

The woman looked at me and smiled. That's when I saw that her mouth was full of little brown and black pegs.

"Give me my brother! and my cat!"

The old woman threw off her cloak and rose up to tower over me. I was afraid the roof might cave in.

If I tell you what was under her cloak, you'd likely die of horror. My brother was in there, screaming, as were other little children. The crone became some hellish thing I might have seen on the movie Poltergeist or House. There was a light calling me to surrender. And all I had was a stupid unicorn horn, which I was pretty sure had no magic in it, to defend myself.

And, that would have been the end. Had I not been smart enough to know better than to disrespect my elders.

What I really did when the old hag came to the counter was brought the pants up there and set them on the glass. Mrs. Partridge just looked at me like a beagle again.

Behind her, the beads continued to sway and swish, which was strange because, well, she was standing here with me. Then I saw another thing that made me sure that my little brother was somewhere in this shop.

An orange and white tail that was all too familiar did a snake-charmers dance and then disappeared through the artificial bones and beads.

I think she may have saw me looking.

"Do you like those, Dear?" she really did have advanced gingivitis, that was no daydream.

Now that I'm writing like my father. And honestly, I never saw myself ending up doing this. Something need be said here about the word 'those'.

I had exactly one pair of pants on the counter, and she was referring to it as plural. Which I guess is just another weird ass thing in this world.

I mean, I have my underwear, but it's called undies. Like there's two.

You could argue that there are holes for both legs so that it's a set, but my t-shirt has three holes, one for a head and two arms, and I don't refer to it as a few.

Whatever. I promise. If anything, my experience with Mrs. Partridge and the hamper of horrors has taught me that you don't have to be on drugs for this world to be weird.

In a few more years, a drink might help me deal with the weird world though, but hey. I'm no advocate.

"Yes, this pair (which is also weird) of pants. I like," I said, refusing to refer to it as a 'them'.

She took the pants and folded them over, to get at the tag. Meaning to snip it and bag it and make the sale. Meanwhile I was looking back over her shoulder.

"Could I see what's back there?" I ventured. Knowing it was useless. Really, I just wanted to gauge her reaction.

A sharpened fingernail pointed to a little red sign above the archway that read exactly what she said to me, "Employees only, Dear."

Well, minus the Dear.

She gave me the eye, again. The milky one, which could make you believe she could see out of it. In reality, she was probably trying to focus her good eye on the tag she was about to snip.

She had that sharpened fingernail taught on the little plastic tab when she paused and brought both eyes up to me.

I thought she may have sensed my intent and was just then gonna transform into whatever thing I had thought up moments before.

But then she said, "How exactly do you intend to pay?"

Which was a really good question to pose because not only was I an invalid, as far as she knew, even though I had dropped that act now, but I was also broke.

Not that I should have to pay even a dollar for my own favorite pants, but the fact that I didn't even have a single buck was simply sad. With that said, if Gabe and I survive all of this, the first thing I am going to do is demand I start getting paid for babysitting.

"Well, Dear?"

I must have been daydreaming.

She put the pants fully down on the counter and put her sun spotted hands flat. I could see that only that one pointer finger had a sharp talon, the rest were nearly bitten to the quick.

"I can't afford to be giving away my treasures."

Followed by Dear, but I think I will spare you that for a while because she said it, like every freaking time.

In fact, it was so much that I imagined she might just have an oven in back and may be stuffing poor Gabe full of gingerbread cookies to fatten him up for dinner.

If so, at least I would know what I had to do. But something was telling me it wouldn't be that easy.

And don't tell me that Mrs. Partridge would have just given a poor girl a dollar pair of blue jeans just because she had given Mom the stinkin' hamper, either. I wouldn't say her charitable, yet thieving donation speaks for her giving heart.

The old woman's fingers began drumming on the glass.

Mom had also bought something that day, though. It was the moth ball smelling blouse! I remembered it. And I had it zipped up in my costume.

"Could I trade in a return?" I blurted, seeing she was at wits end.

Her fingers stopped as I unzipped my uni-onesie part of the way and rummaged inside for the bag.

"There," I said, placing the folded parcel on the counter. "It's still in the bag and it must've cost more than a dollar, or at least that much."

Old Mrs. Partridge didn't even bother taking the blouse out. She used that talon of hers and snipped the price tag off of my jeans, folded them haphazardly and put them in another bag altogether. Sliding it across to me.

She only peeked into the bag, verifying something of possible value were inside and then assumed that beagle stare at me. This time with her head back so that she could look down at me, though she was an inch shorter.

That look said, "If there will be nothing else?"

I took my bag gingerly, not wanting to push my luck any further. At least now, I had some proof, however small.

I dared another glance over her shoulder at the beads and this time I was sure I heard something back there. It could have been Pixie cry, but I swear it sounded like one of Gabe's coos to me.

When she saw me looking, she shifted her head in front of my view and made a sound like a dog on guard. A gruff, huff, if you will.

I don't think my face could hide the fact that I wasn't buying what she was selling, even though, literally I was buying what she was selling. My best effort came out as me taking my sack and first turning my body and then my head toward the exit.

I walked a few paces and then, even though I knew if I looked back, she'd think I was accusing her of something, I did anyway. I just couldn't help it. Gabe was back there.

When I did, I saw the blouse in one of her hands and in the other a gun with two little metal teeth. Before I reached the door to the outside I realized, she was putting one of those little red tags on it.

What would serve her right is if I biked home and reached through the hamper and stole the thing right back!

I was standing outside on the porch in angst watching her shape, behind the stained-glass windows moving from behind the counter and into the room of secondhand clothes.

No doubt to rack the old blouse right back where it started.

Watching that nebulous shadow had my eyes moving the rest of the way along the adobe wall where the porch wrapped around to the back of the building.

Around the back of the house—I'm still calling these shops houses, because that's what they were at some point, and probably still are. I'd bet there's a bedroom somewhere in Nan's Curiosities as well as all the shops down here.

They've only evolved, somehow into the strange establishments they are now. Like living things.

—there was a cellar door. It was slanted, covered in two pieces of plywood, and padlocked. It showed no sign of recent use. Adjacent to it and behind the roots of a banyan tree were the walls of what must've been the employees only area. And out standing on its own in the sandy back lot was a well.

There was even a bucket hanging from a chain, not long enough to be of use, but a sheet of plywood, curled up on the edges was laid across the top of the wells opening to prevent its operation.

I wasn't certain what I meant to do just then. More or less, I was grasping at straws. I could get on my bike and head home. Parents were bound to be home in half an hour anyway, but I just couldn't walk away from this and feel good about myself.

And damn, it was hot.

I was feeling a bit like a Gila monster, standing there in the open of the back lot in the sun. I was in clear view of the road. This is central Florida, there is no foliage worth a damn.

I could only stand there so long in the sun without dying of heatstroke or having someone drive by thinking me lost and looney. In fairness, it wouldn't be far off...

But before I threw in the towel and returned for my bike, Viola came pedaling up the street on her bicycle with training wheels still attached. She must've had a thing for unicorns.

Chapter Nine

I saw the neon lights of her front tire changing into a rainbow as she got nearer. The poor thing must have been eight or nine. Had a little princess flagpole on the bike attached where the training wheels were.

She waved when she saw me standing up on Mrs. Partridge's lot looking lost.

So, I waved back.

Her bike came to a stop down on the sidewalk. Remember, there was no sidewalk leading to the front of Nan's curiosities, but this was the back and she had come down the sidewalk that had reached out toward the Gem Mine.

As it was, she was stopped just down a small slope from me. Anyone who wanted to get into the back lot of Nan's Curiosities without going around would have to climb a minor pylon wall and maneuver through a minefield of succulents.

"What's up?" said VI.

She was wearing a yellow plastic visor, even though which you could see a generous spray of dark freckles across the pale girl's cheeks.

Vi was steadying herself with the tips of her low top converse, either side of her bike, as the training wheels had been adjusted to where they wouldn't be of much help anymore. Her long skinny legs were bloused at the tops under the tight folds of her jean shorts, and her hair was red as can be.

Kid almost reminded her of a lemon popsicle with a smile.

"Well, are you a unicorn are aren't ya?"

That was some statement from such a little thing!

"I'm hot," I said. Just being honest.

The little girl looked just as cozy as if she owned this little corner of the world. Later, I would find out, she kinda did,

"Well, you're not thinking of using that well, I'd hope?"

I gave it a look, a little guilty. I wasn't supposed to be up here, or back here, or whatever.

I swung my arm cooly.

"Nah."

At this point I had braces, and I always heard that they made me prettier, which was weird because that would just be stupid, but when that girl saw the sparkle in my teeth, I thought for a second, my parents might not be totally lying.

Her eyes, just then, reminded me of something you might have seen in a Japanimation. Sailor mooned, all the way. I wasn't one to just make a random friend, but yes, I was one to make a random friend. You kind of learn that skill when you've moved schools three times.

She asked if I wanted some lemonade.

I dared the succulents and hopped down off the treacherous one-foot drop.

"Flat broke," I told her showing her my merch, then zipping it back up in the onesie.

"I wasn't selling it silly!"

Viola backed her bike up like she was making for a three-point turn. Then started toeing it forward inch by inch so I might walk along beside her.

I walked beside her a second, aware I had to go back for my bike eventually. "You sure, because you look like a walking advertisement for a lemonade stand?"

I was teasing, but she was looking down at our shadows while I said it.

"It's cute." I added.

That cheered her up.

"Ah, Mom's got lemonade to spare. I could probably get you in to the gem mine if you wanted, even."

"Actually, I would love some lemonade." I would,

"But, my bike's parked around the front of Nan's."

"It's okay. You can go and get it. I'm not allowed past the end of the walk is all. I live at the Gem Mine House, the one with the water wheel. See?"

She pointed down the way and I suddenly felt excited.

I crunched my way back through the shelly parking lot of Nan's and backed my bicycle out from under the cowl of the huge crab, gripped the handlebars, and set off with Vi.

I know, I should stop here and look back at the shop and promise that I would come back and save my brother and all. But I was thirteen! I had been through a mountain of shit.

Returning home was pending doom. I had not done a single thing I had wanted to do since Mom and Dad walked out that door. And to be true here, I wanted to go to the gem mine. That may have been the only thing that interested me in the whole place!

Vi's mom's house was the coolest house I had ever been inside of.

First off, the front room of the house is a shop with a glass case, kinda like Mrs. Partridge's but without all the creepy sh— tuff.

We're keeping it clean here because now, there's Vi around and, while I'm not the best example for her by sneaking out and losing my kid brother, I could at least watch my language.

The Gem Mine house was welcoming. Totally unlike the crab in the sand, but it still had a grown in look to it that made me feel like there was something more going on here than met the eye.

The entrance had reminded me more of the face of an old-hooded crone, if that makes any sense. Banyan trees were growing in the front lawn and up along the porch. Stretching their roots, or branches, or whatever they were, down like hair around the home.

Underneath you could see the house had been constructed simply with a single steeple, but it stretched back and to the sides. A low stone wall marked the circumference of the property behind, where a few goats we're tied to their poles during business hours, and the water wheel turned.

Along the side of the front entrance, right about where the giant hooded woman's ear would have been, a trail came out from the back yard offering an exit to visitors from the mine. It was covered in gray tarps making it a cave, though in no way threatening, and underneath were the hugest geodes and shards of crystals I had ever seen.

You could see all that approaching the establishment. But once, you had ducked in under the hood of the cheery front entrance and pushed open the glass door, it was a shop.

At first sight, anyway. Vi actually lived there.

Everything was wonderful. Vi didn't seem to notice, but I guess that's what happens with things in life. You just get used to amazing after a while.

The jewels in the case were obviously the most valuable stuff. Tiny diamonds, rough rubies and emeralds, some still growing out of their rocky outcrops. Jewelry, maybe some Vi herself would have helped craft. I didn't know.

It was clean and neat. Vi's mom, Ms. Burchett, was coming through the back door which was easily seen from the front door. The door she came through was a wooden six-panel type with glass panes so I could see straight through to the Gem Mining that was going on behind the house.

But she had obscured it at first coming through to greet us.

"Hello."

Ms. Burchett's voice was so welcoming. Maybe she was treating me like a customer? I'm not sure if she treats customers and normal people differently actually.

But, that would mean that there are perfect people in this world then, wouldn't it? Still, I always think of Ms. Burchett when I see someone being sour. And it helps.

"Hi," I said.

Vi was looking up at me, already trying to imitate the smile I give with my braces. Why do people do that?

"Well, Vi? Who's your new friend."

Ms. Burchett slid behind the counter by the front door and perched on a stool there. She was completely not what I expected. She must have had Vi when she was my age!

She had a small frame and her hair in a pony. Was wearing Timberland's boots, cut-off overalls, and had what looked like a toolbelt around her waist. Only there wasn't any tools in it, just a big tan leather pocket.

It was around then that I lost all track of time. The sun was still shining. Kids were back there gem mining. I had two glasses of lemonade and I was feeling like I kinda belonged somewhere for the first time in a long time. People were nice.

This was a total turnaround from my initial impressions of the Art District, I mean, I had passed some pretty shady characters on the way here, but now that I was here, it was kinda like our house.

And, I hate to be repetitive and a little bit punny, but it was another diamond in the rough!

I was standing there listening to Vi and her mom, who talked to her more like a friend, blabber about something that had occurred while some customers were cleaning off their findings or whatnot, when I saw something a little bit out of place.

It was a Christmas tree.

I had wandered over to one of the open rooms adjacent to the entrance. There were two or three smaller rooms, I guess you'd call them. They displayed different types of things.

I say two or three because the third room was just kind of the exit room going out from the entrance to the back. The door swung in on that room so that made for most of the space there, but even that wall had a peg board with hand-crafted necklaces hanging from it.

The room I was in had the Christmas tree on a dais in the middle of the floor. If I didn't know any better, and I didn't, I would say that when Christmas came knocking, this would likely be the place Santa deposited his gifts. Of course, the shop would be closed and playing its part as their private home for that occasion.

That was so freakin' cool! For them to live like that.

So much for seeing what's right in front of your face. Man how time flies!

I could write a whole nother book about Vi's place and maybe one day I will, but when she took me into her home I just felt like life could be better.

That everyone could leave their doors open during the day and let the sunshine through and the people through, and then at night get all cozy and warm and family-like. Boy, had I been missing something that Vi had not.

But, it was at that particular moment when that miniature glass Christmas tree caught my eye, that I started to bring things together about all that portal opening and closing stuff that had thus far seemed too nauseating to tackle.

I walked around the tree in that room as Vi and her Mom/bff chatted away, feeling more than a little jealous.

I was trying to figure out what was so different about it, that it had been placed here like it had. It seemed to be made all of glass.

It was definitely made all of glass. The star on top was right even with my forehead, Dad would say fivehead, and why I thought of that just now I couldn't tell you. But the tree was only about three feet tall, because it was sitting on that pedestal.

The glass was painted green like any Christmas fir tree and indeed it was pretty. At the tip of each glass-blown fur-point there was a light of different color. Which made the Christmas tree sparkle. The rest of the ornaments that were on the tree had been blown into the glass and stained or painted to perfection.

But the very tips of each bough were what twinkled.

Upon closer scrutiny, I was beginning to see that it was little birds that had lit on each tip of the giant ornamental fir tree.

"We chopped it down ourselves!" Vi yelled, over the sound of water falling when someone had opened the backdoor of the shop again. She was right on top of me again.

I'm telling you; she would have mined my braces straight from my mouth.

"Chopped what down?" I asked.

Okay, so some things just go right over my head. Guilty. I never said I was the brightest light on the, er, tree or whatever.

"Oh my Gosh! Never mind!" She bopped around the tree to the other side and then I finally got it.

"Ohh! You're funny." I said trying to recover. She wagged her head from side to side like it was no biggie.

"This is your Christmas tree?" I asked, feeling even more dumb when the words came out of my mouth.

She settled a bit and looked up at it.

"It doesn't look like much now, but once the gifts are under it, it looks like a real tree, and Mom always sticks some real pine sprigs in there with the Christmas gifts, so it feels and smells like it's alive."

"I think it's beautiful." I said, making to touch one of the little twinkling birds. When my finger touched it, the bird wiggled and nearly fell from its perch.

I panicked and took my hand back hoping I didn't break anything.

"Crap!"

The once blue little bird, as it had temporarily winked out, settled back into its perch and glowed again, then, Vi laughed.

"Don't worry. They're supposed to do that—"

She reached up and drew the little bluebird right off its perch and into her hand. Attached to it was a long glass stilt. And where it had been was left a little hole for the stilt shining through with now white light.

I was shocked. Then I reached out and took one of the other little birds like she had, this time a red one. It was tiny in my hand. Crystal and pink, wings spread.

Vi held hers up to me like a wine glass toast and laughed.

Now two white dots slowly spun on the center dais at the tip of the glass tree's fir boughs.

"Mom says, and it's a legend really, but she believes that this is how the big crystal works."

"The big crystal?" I asked uncertainly. Spinning my little bird in my fingers.

"Yeah! You saw the ones in the exit tunnel? Those aren't found by kids out back in the shaker stall. Downstairs is the good stuff."

I was looking at her as if she were from some other planet.

"You see the light bulb in there? The one inside the tree right?"

"You mean in the Christmas tree?"

"Yeah. The white light in the center is the real power. All the other little crystals, like these birds are just waypoints. Filters or colors, you see?" She put her bird back on the tree and it went blue again.

I was genuinely perplexed.

And she must have picked up on it because she took my hand and dragged me toward the back door. I had to tug her to me and reach to plug my own little bird back into the tree before I let her haul me away.

I could see kids beyond the back door sifting their buckets of sand in hopes of finding some treasure. But right before she opened the back door to the outside, she hit the peg board on the wall with her left hand and a trapdoor opened beneath it that all of sucked us right into it.

I had to duck beneath the pegboard which I now realized was the upper half of an old saloon style swinging door. The steps were so steep I was practically dragged downward by Vi's little hand when she took them so fast.

The wooden steps had been at an angle more appropriate for a ladder, but they were wide enough that I didn't have to use my hands. Good thing since Vi had one of them.

We were in their unfinished basement. Unfinished is a word I use lightly, as it was the first basement I had ever seen that still had a dirt floor and stone walls on three of the sides.

It was dark down there now that the trap door had slammed shut above us. Behind the steps I could see the outside of the house, as strange as that sounds. There was definitely vinyl siding behind the ladder thingy, yet we were underground. The ceiling was entirely made of the roots of the huge banyan tree suggesting that this little cave had been here forever.

Vi let go of my hand and was reaching for the chain of a bare-naked lightbulb hanging from the ceiling. The floor was already sloping slightly away and she was on her tippy toes.

I helped her out.

"Thanks. Mom always moves the crate."

Then I could see the far side of the basement where the roots dove back into the dirt and stone. Beneath that, the cavern extended down, the walls sparkling from the new light. Either they were wet, or something more fantastic.

"Mind your head here at the first part," said Vi. "The stone doesn't give an inch." She didn't have to duck. I did.

I would have never believed this existed so close to my house. Yes, the sign had said Gem Mine, but I assumed it was a shop and a place to let kids have a little fun. Not, a literal gem mine!

Chapter Ten

On the left of the cave entrance there were two workbenches. Identical to one another in every way besides their size. One was Vi-sized, and the other Ms. Burchett sized.

Vi took a toolbelt, similar to her mothers, from the tabletop and put it on.

From the rack between the workstations, she took a couple of plastic flashlights and handed me one.

Down on the ground below was a shoe rack with two sets of dusty work boots and next to them a pair of leather shoes with the toes worn out of them.

Vi exchanged her tennis shoes for her boots then snatched a metal flashlight that was much too big for her (my mom calls those kinds the hit you over the head flashlights) and slipped it into the hammer loop of her toolbelt.

She turned on her little plastic job and shook it to life.

"More reliable," she said, patting the mag lite.

The lighting was pretty decent as it was. Yellowing bulbs pocked the right-hand wall every thirty feet or so but the cavern that stretched down wasn't entirely straight.

I think she registered the slight worry in my eyes.

"Don't worry," she said. "There's only one place where it is kinda iffy. But that's the best part!"

Her glasses had a mist on them, and she wiped them with a cloth from her toolbelt pouch.

"How far does it go?" I asked.

"Not far."

She stepped ahead of me.

"And, you own all of this?"

"Well, Mom says Grandpa used to say it's Earth and you can't own the land just because you're standing on it. But, it *is* under our house." Slowly she started down.

Though most of the walls were smooth, teeth of quartz and amethyst jutted out at odd angles. Sometimes Vi would put her hand on an egg-shaped stone and point out that it was probably crystal inside.

"So, this is where you mined everything in the shop?" I asked, edging around a slippery corner.

There was no real danger, besides of getting wet, as a shallow pool curved along just below the stone path we followed.

"Well, mining isn't legal in this, whatcha macallit? Presinct? No that's police. Well, it isn't allowed here. At least not machinery."

The path widened out and became a little flatter now.

"Okay?" I said stating the obvious contradiction.

She shined her flashlight down, drawing my attention to a steel cable now running along on our left about two feet off the ground. It was drawn tight through eyelets atop steel posts.

"This thing won't keep anyone from climbing over, just don't trip. Steel splinters are not fun," she said.

I decided to give my flashlight a go.

"Then how do you get away with it? The mining I mean?"

"Well," she shined the flashlight in her own face and looked back, "I'm about to show you."

She smiled and then turned back following the cable. I started to hear a faint trickle of water.

We were coming up on something that looked like a piece of machinery off to our left and I mentioned as much to Vi.

"Not machinery," said she. "This baby uses good ole fashioned elbow grease."

Beyond the steel cable dropped a pit in the stone. The machinery thingy had a couple of pulleys hanging from some tackle on an arm made of steel frame, the pieces bolted together. A chain and steel cable, like the one that made the barrier, stretched down into the dark of the abyss.

On this side of the barrier was the majority of the working parts of the winch; A hand crank and a lever. Those looked to lock the crane in place over the drop.

We stopped at the winch, and she turned to me with her flashlight down.

"Would you believe me if I said the gems just kinda pop-up?"

Behind her, I could see that the tunnel went on a bit further, and I could hear the trickle of water down there, but most astonishing was what was lining the wall beyond.

All along the walls, from here on, were stones of different colors, shapes, and sizes. My flashlight lit them up one-by-one like those birds on the Christmas tree.

"Yeah," said Vi nonchalant. "That's what mom calls 'The Cache'. It's where we pile them up. Nothing magical about that though. Take a look if you want."

I took a few paces into where the cavern opened up to a dead-end chamber that stretched up in the dark. A thin waterfall was emptying here into a sparkling pool of tiny jewels, and around the pool and behind the waterfall was what I can only describe as a dragon's fortune.

They weren't piles of gold. But, stones and gems, that must have been just as valuable, if not more valuable, were everywhere. I mean, I was only thirteen when I saw, so a lot of the rocks were most likely tiger's eyes, or fool's gold, or opal, but ya know opal's can be worth a fortune!

There were piles of the stuff in and around the pool that ended the tunnel, and of course, there were geodes; those rock-egg thingies that have crystals inside of them.

It was kept kinda neat, really, I didn't get the impression that they were wasteful people, and I wouldn't have thought that anyway. Looking back, it was exactly what I would have done in their situation.

Nothing moved, besides the clear pool where the water fell. I thought to myself if I had moved a single stone then I might cause a wave of colorful pyrites to cascade down the side of one of the mounds into the pool.

There was a wheelbarrow parked on the right of the falls and a wooden shovel that was more of a tube than a spoon.

As it were, I was just standing there at the slope down to the mouth of the pool, staring. Vi's flashlight beam was coming over my shoulder so that my shadow, though dim, was staring back at me from the far wall.

The shadow of a freaking unicorn standing here, in a cave of wonders!

I thought of watching the Last Unicorn and being worried that Schmindrick the magician was going to lose his love, and the Unicorn was going to lose her magic, and that everyone was going to lose something.

Then I thought of Gabe, and that he might be trapped like the other unicorns right now, by the red bull. And I realized, there was something I was more afraid of than anything else.

Being alone.

The light flickered and the shadow of my horn wavered back at me.

"Tanner?"

It was Vi.

"Would you believe me?" she asked. "Would you believe me if I told you that the gems just kinda popped up?"

I walked up to where she stood next to the crane and said, "Would you believe me if I told you something?"

I was about at the part about Gabe being eaten by the Hamper, which was actually the cat chewing a dinosaur nugget, when Vi was finishing up cranking the payload out from the pit.

That's when she rudely interrupted.

I had to give it to her though, she had been nodding and saying, uh huh, with her tongue sticking out of the side of her mouth the whole time, all while having her boot planted on the steel cable and cranking that thing up all along. Now it had reached the top.

"You see now how it's all white light down there?" She asked motioning for me to look beneath the plywood deck that was strung up before us.

The plywood was wrapped in a metal mesh, far beyond rusted, and was held aloft by a chain bound to each corner with bolts and washers. At its center was a stone in the shape of an ostrich egg, surrounded by smaller stones of varying colors and shapes.

I was giving her a late nod when she said,

"Watch it," pulling a lever and swiveling the platform over to the cave floor.

I stepped back and the thing looked like it was going to fit nicely into an indention, obviously made from this same motion for time unimagined. It did fit and it was loud.

Vi wasn't gentle when she dropped the payload. The little gear she'd been cranking on wound out three loud clicks that had barely started their echo when the platform hit the stone and washed it out.

"Now, now, now," Vi's voice caught the back end of the sound and came back echoing since she had spoken up. "There's, there's the little birdie, birdie, birdie."

The pit still shimmered with its white light and the stones on the platform now had only a phosphorescent glow.

Vi took off some leather gloves that I had failed to see her put on during my mesmerizing meeting with the cave of wonders. While she was approaching me and the platform, she shoved them into the pouch of her toolbelt.

"See them?" she said, meaning the small cache of valuables she had cranked up from below.

"Yeah," I said, letting the hand drop that had been shielding my eyes from the brightness of the well, which was just then beginning to dim a little.

Vi, crouched down on the platform and waved for me to join her.

She rolled the big egg-shaped rock onto its wider side, "Geode," then she picked up a silver stone with a triangular shape eyeing it, "Hematite." Putting that stone back down she grabbed up a piece of fool's gold and another smaller stone of sparkly gray and white, "Pyrite and rock crystal."

She tossed them down thoughtlessly and looked up at me.

"It's random."

She was looking at me. Working out just how much she was going to have to explain. I'm sure my face didn't offer her any decent starting point, so I just reached down and picked up the little piece of rock crystal and studied it.

When Vi finally seemed to settle on something, she stood up and walked over to where she could prop an elbow on the edge of the winch assembly and stare down into the now dimly lit pit without much effort.

I got up with her and approached its edge again, daring another look.

"At first, it wasn't lit up like that, because the bottom was covered in stones."

Vi hiked an elbow at the cave of wonders where the waterfall spilt down among the piles of jewels, "All that. Besides what we sell, ya know?"

When she paused, I took the opportunity to study the bottom of the pit and could see that it was entirely made of milky quartz.

She continued, "Once everything was cleared out, new stones would just appear in the bottom of the well."

I looked up at the ceiling run amok with stalagmites, but otherwise solid stone.

"First thought, right?" Vi said, smiling with her bright white teeth and pointing to the ceiling. "But no one's dropping things in from a wishing well." She took her glasses off this time and gave them a good wiping on her shirt. "Not some garden gnome toting emeralds over from the cache at the falls, either. We thought that for a few days. What else we're we to think?" She paused a moment. "Mom said, she'd have people believe we had the seven dwarfs down here mining for us first."

I had to admit, the thought had crossed my mind.

Vi put her glasses back on and said, "It's like this. If we're looking, nothing happens. So we devised this platform system that would go down and cover up most of the light. Now, only a few little things show up, never more. If it isn't moved, nothing else comes through."

I was thinking about my cat coming out of the hamper on night number one, smelling of Mrs. Partridge. Vi probably saw that I was thinking, or at least assumed I was trying to follow. I think I surprised the heck out of her when I said, "Can you send it back?"

"What?" she asked. "Why would we want to do that?" Then she looked confused and a little out of her element, "I mean, I don't think so."

The light from the well was fading more now and the waterfall filled the silence for a moment.

"Why would you ask that, Tanner?"

I was thinking of how I had pulled that red onesie through the hamper before I had turned and looked.

"Do you think there could be others?" I asked without giving her time to answer. "Pop-up points, I mean. Do you think Mrs. Partridge, I mean Nan, could have one under her shop of curiosities?"

She looked baffled. And then, I was baffled when I saw a tear form under those glasses, right in the corner of her eye.

"Are you saying… you believe me?" she said.

"Are you kidding?" I told Vi, grabbing her gently by both shoulders and shaking her playfully.

"Haven't your heard I word I've been saying?"

She crossed her arms after wiping her eyes.

"You mean about your Insta whatever?"

"Instagram! But, that's not what it's about. It's about my brother! I think she has him!"

Then I took her by the hand and started heading back up the way we had come. "Now, *I* have something to show *you*."

Chapter Eleven

I had pretty much filled her in on everything by the time we were crossing the little sandlot and succulent mine field toward the back of Mrs. Partridge's.

Yes, I'm calling her Mrs. Partridge.

It turned out that leaving the gem mine was no big deal. Vi's mom was as cool as a cucumber.

I'm not dissing my parents, but they always assume I'm up to no good. Had I come out of a secret trapdoor with a stranger, they'd have gone postal.

But, at Vi's house, when we came out of the trap door thing and went by Ms. Burchett, she was ringing up a customer.

As I had passed her, she gave me a little look that was soon masked by a giant bubble she had been blowing with her chewing gum.

I took another sideways glance at the strange Christmas tree, now understanding a bit more, and heard the gum pop on our way out of the door.

Now, Vi and I were on our bellies peering through the basement window at the back of Nan's Curiosities. The window was half buried in the sand like the landscape had been built around the shop rather than the other way around.

Vi was rubbing a circle of mold from the glass with the sleeve of her yellow shirt. Her freckly cheeks all wrinkled up as she squinted to see in.

"I think we've found her cache."

Inside, beyond my own pink reflection, I could see that there were piles of wares.

Her basement was finished, resembling the decor of the front entryway. Two steps led down from what could have been the same beaded doorway I'd seen inside. But the walls in the basement had tiles of assorted colors embedded in the adobe. Large ones. Red, yellow, orange. Each with a rim of gray stucco.

It reminded me of a Spanish restaurant, minus the food. But it had everything else you could imagine.

A rocking horse barely stood out in a pile of random wooden carvings that were in such a tangle you could hardly tell their forms.

Another pile across the room consisted of what seemed to be chains, and strings. What might have been a windchime peeked out from among other copper-tinged candelabra, and brass rods, maybe for curtains.

Against one wall was a giant shelf of cubby holes made of wood and stuffed full of all sorts of things one might find in a shop of curiosities. The shelf was far too large to have been brought in by the door and must have been constructed inside of the room itself.

Our view was obscured beyond where the ground met the window, but it gave the overall impression of an inundated collector.

"She has one, Vi!" I said, searching for the correct word for it.

Vi looked at me while I stammered, trying to describe a wormhole without a having P.H.D. in physics.

"A, a… A perch! Like those birds. She has a perch made of light in there somewhere, I know it!"

"I like it," said Vi nodding sideways in the dirt. "A perch. Just to think, a pop-up spot that brought you anything you wanted!"

I thought about it and was having a hard time getting excited about it despite Vi's encourageable expression. Then I took another peek inside at the piles and said, "It looks like it brings her a lot of things she doesn't want as well."

Then Mrs. Partridge came through the beads and into the basement, her gaze most definitely directed right to my little buried window. But I had ducked my head away quickly and Vi was already away and getting to her knees.

Still uncertain, I hurried her away, pecking our way back across the minefield of cacti and down the street, until we both were safely at the crossroads of the 'Art District'.

What can I say? It was growing on me. Mom would be proud.

The Death of Science

Kristen was sitting there with her back against the wall, flipping the pages of her creative writing journal back and forth. She thought she was starting to see the bigger picture. Curiously, Tanner had stopped with her narrative, and she could hear Death down there possibly toeing that yoyo again.

So, if I have this straight, she thought, not knowing if Death was reading her mind or not at this point, these pop-up spots may very well be the reason that no one cleaned up this area after the great flood?

She waited to see if Death would impose on her private conversation with herself, but he didn't. So, she continued to pretend that it wasn't any more nuts to be talking to herself than it was to be talking to the incarnation of Death and continued right along.

Maybe that was when the whole science was dead thing started!

But why wasn't this place under lock and key. You'd think there would be half a dozen spells on this property to keep people from mucking around with it.

"Ah, ah, ah," said Death from down below.

So he *was* in her head! "They just say that in school, Kristen," he said. "Science is not dead. On the contrary, he's finding new life in Rootworld."

Oh God, another Incarnation, she thought, but then she felt he might have been playing with her. She thought about the Memorial Skybridge, which used to be the Skyway before the collapse, and how none of the minors were allowed to cross without special visas and how their experience of the internet was always confined to local searches.

"Your own text book says it best," said the Reaper man, "It wouldn't be right to start kids off out there in the real world where Magic and Science both flow freely. Not, without letting them first learn to live a little more ordinarily."

Then she thought, come to think of it, their introduction to magic classes did seem a little bit lacking in the earlier years...

"Believing in Magic couldn't kill Science any more than believing in the Devil could kill God," said Death boldly, and Kristen jerked around to look at his face. She thought she saw the coins in his eyes stop spinning for a second.

"Just relax, Kristen, there's time," Death said. Then Kristen thought about it for a moment and became confused as to whether he was talking about the dimension or the personification.

"You'll get your Visa. It's really a no-fail system of education anymore. Shame if you ask me. Children used to have respect for their elders."

"Ugh," she scoffed, "you're starting to sound like my father!"

Death would have looked aghast at that statement if he wasn't always looking aghast. He hardly could remember his own father but was reasonably sure his dad did say something of the sort to him before. Maybe he *was* starting to get a little old.

"Inside of these Rearing Domes, inbound teleportation is all that's permitted. You see, these pop-up points let you in, and with some exceptions, there are connections within the domes to places inside of the domes themselves, but outside of the domes, well..."

He sighed, and Kristen thought he may be getting aggravated again. She decided to drop it for now.

"It's okay," she said, jotting in her notebook. "I think I understand. Please, I'm ready to continue."

He took in a breath that sounded like he was apologetic. Then Kristen heard a light tapping by the rim of the window behind where she sat jotting. She spun and looked.

Death was rapping on the glass below ground level with the blade of his sickle in order to get her attention. He seemed to regain his serenity as the scythe's wooden handle tocked gently on the floor by his foot.

"You'll see. Just as our story turns out. Things out there in the real world, have a way of returning."

Once again, Death's voice turned to Tanner's in her head.

Down the street to Vi and I's left there was a terrible screeching coming from a screened in lanai that let out on to a rocky lawn. We both looked that direction in time to see a wiry man in a pin-striped suit dragging, what looked to be an easel, out toward the road.

"Ye gads," I said.

In the man's yard was a sculpture made from hubcaps and clothes hangers, among other things.

The man parked the easel on the sidewalk and the tiny rusty wheel finally stopped screaming. Then, he unfolded it into a complete workstation with bench and all. Only then did we see his face as he dusted off his hands.

He was a bit far off, but the gaunt features combined with his two front teeth combined to impress a very jovial demeanor.

He saw us looking his direction and saluted, then did a Michael Jackson type of jig.

I looked at Vi who seemed to be enjoying it and then back to the strange man.

From inside of the house, I heard a woman's voice, "There's three of these to put out you handsome man! You just come back in here and make sure you let me know when to watch you carry them out!"

He looked back at us after showing a bit of alarm in the voice's direction, shook his hands and arms like he was relinquishing a character facade and then marched back into the lanai.

Something about that voice was familiar. It was the kind of voice that Oprah Winfrey would use while she passed out free love gifts. Welcoming. Energetic. Inclusive; as in, loud enough for the world to hear.

"That's Spock," said Vi, "and Mott."

Vi hop-scotched the first few sidewalk blocks to where our bikes were laying, "Let me introduce you."

I looked back up toward the cellar doors, adjacent the buried window, before I felt Vi tug at my sleeve.

"C'mon. If the old witch saw ya, it will be a good spot to get forgotten."

I turned down the final unexplored road marked by the green arrow, reading ARTIST and hop-scotched my own way toward more mystery.

Chapter Twelve

The Art District had officially been the epitome of crossroads everywhere.

I mean, in life you sometimes come to a crossroads. In love, same. While walking and biking, literal, crossroads. I had ventured down every pointed way along these crossroads, and let's face it.

This could make one heck of a choose your own adventure story, but I just don't have that in me.

Not after Spock and Mott.

These two, had this been a choose your own adventure story, would have been the first logical choice. But if you'd gone that way you would always lead yourself back to where you started.

That's how this road is. And that's because that's how these two characters are. They are a circle. One leads to another and the other to the other until everything is covered in orange and pink paint. And the car is rebranded and there's new signs on the telephone poles. And the dog has a new haircut.

Okay. The dog was actually cute. It was one of those little Pomeranians, but it was trimmed like a lion. It had a mane and a little tail fluff but that was about it.

Its name, I would find out later, would be, Mr. Bigglesworth.

When I first shook hands with Spock, I thought I may be meeting the real live Mad Hatter, as hair was springing from his nose and ears in grey bunches.

The hair on his head was a combination of gold and grey that stood up an entire foot and formed the shape of an unremovable top hat. His front teeth would give you the impression of Mr. Rabbit, but not because they were buck teeth, but rather his whole top row of teeth were prominent when he spoke.

He seemed to know Vi, for the most part, though I was never entirely sure. When he shook my hand and she introduced me, the exchange was so quick I hardly thought he had time to notice, much less remember my name.

However, he swiftly gave my hand a pronounced upward and downward tug, and then marveled at the unicorn outfit I was in.

"You see," he said waving his hands theatrically as he was again bound toward the screened in area, which I could now see led into quite a roomy little studio, "Mott! Magic is in the air."

He looked back momentarily before retreating into the ranch style architecture and said pointedly, "I told her that magic was in the air."

We'd left our bikes at the sidewalk where Spock had been setting up the easels for some 'light painting', and were following him down the footpath which became pink sandstone block and then, when underground, adobe.

Once we realized we had stepped under the screened porch and into an adobe studio with windows cut straight from the earthen walls, that voice came again, like Oprah Winfrey's.

"Oh, you beautiful white man, you just keep doing what you're doin' and the magic will happen."

Now, if I told you Mother Goose existed in real life. You probably wouldn't believe me. And you wouldn't believe me if I told you she was a six foot and two-inch black woman with a smile and eyes as white as snow. But the woman that came from her personal rooms into that studio area, wearing a one size too big body suit and platform shoes, sure reminded me of what Mother Goose might well look like had she been born in the Art District. And Spock, well. He was either her husband, or her friend. I couldn't figure it out, but she loved him either way.

"Vi!" exclaimed Mott, reaching out and hugging her.

Temporarily Vi disappeared somewhere inside of Mott's bosom. Once she emerged, Mott was walking past to inspect Spock's handywork all while carrying on with Vi.

"Did you ever get me those gemstones we were talking about, Honey?"

Vi turned on a dime and followed the exuberant woman up her hallway and back out into the light under the screened in area.

"Mom, says to come down anytime during the day and she will let you pick any of the best stuff."

Mott turned back, all but yelling over Vi's head and my shoulder, "Spock you perfect man-thing, I love it! Put the canvases out here and start with the time that little girl met Jim Dandy and they did that dancing thing."

Mott put the back of her hand under her chin, as if she were framing for a photo and asked Vi, "And your momma's still agreed to put my bookmarks on her counter when I release my book next week?"

Vi was shaking her head, trying to catch up to the speed of things in this household. Then Mott turned her attention to me.

"You child. I love it. Is Halloween back again already?"

"Just passed, actually," I said, unsure what to say.

"Oh, I see." Said Mott, showing that big, beautiful smile, "You're just making a statement." She winked at me and said, "Get it girl."

We followed Mott back out of the sun and into the shade of the underground studio. Spock sidled by with Mr. Bigglesworth on a leash and three large canvases underarm.

"I was gonna say," started Mott.

"I have all this work to get rid of from last Halloween. It couldn't be here already." She lifted a casual hand to bring our attention to the passing artwork on the walls. All of it nicely framed, even if everyone kinda looked the same.

We seemed to be following Mott down a hallway that ended at a door. Off to the left was a room, much like a living room but for more people, perhaps. The confidence Mott was walking with made me hope the fast-approaching door was going to open of its own accord, lest she may run right into it.

Then Vi said, just in time to stop her, "Did you paint all of these?"

The tall woman did an about face.

"Lord no, child." She smacked her lips and batted her eyelashes, which now I could see were extra-long. "Spock is the artist. I do all of the writing."

Mott leaned down more to our level and told us a secret, under only slightly hushed tones- normal volume for the average human.

"Ever heard a picture's worth a thousand words?"

We nodded to one another.

"Well, don't believe it girls. Not for a second."

Mott stepped back between us and turned right into the sitting room.

In the center of the room was a coffee table situated before a long curving leather sofa. She reached beneath the lip of the table and placed a few canvas paintings out for our admiration. Then, with some effort, found her feet again just long enough to turn and drop herself into a giant easy chair obviously made just for her.

We were looking over the paintings.

All three were of the same little black girl. One had her standing before a big tree, another had her by a pond with a frog and the last had her sitting on a rolled bale of hay.

Mott looked totally relaxed for about three seconds, then she sat forward and slid a mess of papers in a wooden three ring binder from the top of her chair-side table.

It had been a marvel that the heavy thing was propped atop its three skinny copper legs to begin with.

She added the book to the coffee-table paintings and said, "Every picture needs a good story. It gives it value."

I thought we may be getting ourselves into a history lesson and glanced back over my shoulder from the couch and out of the French window. Though most of the top panes were obscured with English ivy growing wildly, I could see Spock out there in the sun.

He had a paintbrush dripping with yellow, working joyfully at an easel, all while doing an Irish dance of sorts to keep Mr. Bigglesworth from tangling his feet up in the leash.

I chuckled.

Vi had opened the book, turning over the sometimes-fragile pages one by one. Though, far from ready for the press, it was Mott's manuscript. Every bit was handwritten with photos of Spock's paintings paper clipped in strategic places throughout.

I sat down on the floor with Vi to get a closer look.

"How long did it take to write all of this?" I asked.

"Well, let's see," Mott said, sitting forward and putting her elbow on her knee and her forefinger in her mouth to think. "Forty-two years, about," she smiled matter-of-factly, "not including a few months during the first chapter when Momma was expecting me to arrive soon."

She looked at her nails then rested her chin on her knuckles watching us patiently survey the huge work, perhaps hoping for a positive reaction.

Not likely with Vi folding the pages back now in chunks. But then, more than halfway through the huge volume, Vi came across a photograph she thought she recognized.

"Is this a painting of the Lumpin Family Circus?"

"Sure is!" said Mott. "You'd not believe that old lot across the way became that painting you see. But, once a year for the last twenty years, it brought people from miles around." Then she looked a little thoughtful and the corners of her mouth briefly turned down, "Well, all but last year." Then her smile sparkled again like she'd never said it.

I glanced back out past Spock and Mr. Bigglesworth at the barren lot. Was it true? Had I been sitting on a bleacher seat right there under a tent not more than two years prior. I had. Just waiting to meet my little brother.

It all seemed so long ago.

"That is a rendition of one of the first times they set up here. I was just turning twenty and nothing stole my heart more than Cracker Jacks and cotton candy. Well, nothing but David Copperfield."

Both of us just kinda looked at one another when we saw Mott looking out the window at Spock. Still kinda wonder if she meant the Broadway Magician Copperfield or the Earnest Hemmingway Copperfield. Something told me that maybe it was both. Maybe she found her Hemmingway in her writing and her magic in Spock.

Vi flipped the page and there was another ancient painting, this one of the Gem Mine.

"And that," Mott said with renewed interest, "was my first visit to the Gem Mine after your mom inherited the responsibility."

Vi's eyes went a little glassy. Mott noticed.

"Did you know I used to visit that shop when I was just a little bity Mott? You're Grandfather ran it then."

Vi perked up a little, still shyly turning adjacent pages back and forth hoping to find more paintings or photos.

Mott sat back in her easy chair and Mr. Bigglesworth came running in and hopped right up into her lap with the leash trailing him. She hardly took notice and just stroked the little lion.

"Good ole, Mr. Burchett." she said. "Wasn't a nice little stone mining set-up back then. No. That was your momma's doing I'd reckon. Mr. Burchett had a different angle."

Mr. Bigglesworth started licking at Mott's face and Mott could see Vi was touched by the memory of her grandfather.

At that point, Spock entered under the archway of the sitting room, his pin-striped suit covered in yellow paint. He didn't seem to mind. Just stood there with his odd smile, obviously only concerned with his puppy who had escaped.

Mott handed Bigglesworth to Vi who put him in her lap and started petting him. Then Mott gave Spock a look that assured him the dog was fine.

Spock started ticktocking his hips and tapping his foot then put his arms out and said, "What's black and white and yellow all over?" Then he did a shimmy and danced in a turn with his fingers pointing toward the top of his own head.

He was about to depart, but when I saw he wasn't going to offer more of a punch line I said, "A chicken zebra!"

He danced a few pointed fingers my way in appreciation and went right back out to his painting. I think he got it. I was totally glad someone did.

Mott was back to her story.

"Mr. Burchett was quite the magician. I once watched him blow bubbles at a magic show that he plucked right out of the air. When he handed them out to us, they were solid stone right from his gem shop."

Vi smiled a little. Then dared a few words about her grandpa.

"Mom doesn't like talking about him, it makes her sad."

"Terrible loss, Mr. Burchett. But I will tell you something special. He always wore the same shoes. Said he'd bought them from a man in Ecuador and liked them so much that he purchased as many pairs as would last him the rest of his life."

Mott turned a few pages back and showed us a bold heading. One of the chapters was called, Mott and the old shoes.

"During his final year of performances, he told everyone that he would be disappearing soon, as the shoes on his feet were his very last pair. And anyone who knew anything would tell you, the socks stuck right out from the front of his old shoes that year before he died. I remember, always his big toe was showing through a hole in the socks. Sometimes, I thought maybe he just liked his socks that way."

Vi had a tear in her eye.

I couldn't stop thinking about those old shoes in Vi's basement.

While the two were caught up in old memories, I saw something among the pages of Mott's manuscript. It was an old photograph of a Halloween festival right there in the district, probably during the same time Vi's mom had taken over the Gem Mine.

In the photograph, glowing pumpkins were strung on lines along the sidewalk. Paper bags lined the street curb. One kid on a wooden scooter was pushing along. But the background was what caught my attention.

It was unmistakable. The backyard of Nan's Curiosities and, the well.

Chapter Twelve

On the page of the book, a bright light was coming up from the well, giving the whole Halloween photograph a festival glow. Even in black and white.

"Vi!" I said, quite alarming both of them. Then I pointed to the photograph.

She was registering the finding when Mott said, "Oh that's one my Spocky baby hasn't gotten 'round to yet."

Then she leaned a little closer to pet the little lion again, "Truth is, I like to stretch out the painting he does. Ya know? Save the best for last, because—" she sat back, "—oh, how I do love to see the beautiful man work."

A sound came from her like a hiccup of self-surprise and desire, the silky curls of her hair bouncing.

Mott was lounging, looking very content for once when Vi asked her, "Is this the well behind Nan's shop from way back then?"

"Sure was," Mott said. "And that reminds me. Nan's been around just as long. She used to play along when the circus came to town too. It was a regular three ring type. They all had acts."

Bigglesworth wiggled free from Vi's clutches, and I turned over some more of the yellowed parchment. There in a photo was Mrs. Partridge. A much younger Mrs. Partridge, but I would recognize those teeth and that bob from anywhere!

She had both arms out like the items out in front of her shop were the cat's meow. And right next to her was an elderly man beaming a perfect smile of much better teeth than her own.

"Grandpa?" said Vi.

Mott stood up and swept up the big 'ole book into her arms and clapped it shut, the old photo of Nan and Grandpa twirling out from it and on to the floor. Mott didn't notice, instead she held the considerable folder tight against her bosom. Her head cocked up in reminiscence and pride.

"Oh yes. One of the acts that your Grandpa used to put on when the circus was in town was quite a riot. Had the whole district in an uproar for two seasons. Still don't know how they done it."

Vi and I were rapt.

Mott putt the huge volume back on the flimsy copper table without much regard, but it stood perfectly balanced the first try. Then she began tidying up the paintings and stowing them back under the coffee table.

Vi had secretly picked up the photograph.

When Mott was satisfied, she looked at the two of us who were now sitting on the sofa staring.

"Well?" she said. Her beautiful lips and eyes giving no sign that she had left us hanging on a total cliff. "What da ya think?"

Vi went to blurt out the obvious question but I beat her to the punch hoping not to offend our quirky host.

"It's wonderful!" I squealed.

Mott was struck in total silence for a moment just measuring me up. And at that moment, I felt like I had been in her position before.

I remembered being at a talent show. Mom and I had practiced my dance over and over, got me the right clothes, everything. Dad had psyched me up like I was the bomb.

Of course, Mom and Dad were down there watching me along with all the other parents but, what I was putting on was a little in-your-face and I had to perform it out in front of everyone, even my classmates were sitting on stage waiting their turn.

My worst fear was that no one would clap or say a single thing when I was all done, because I knew that it was just not a normal routine and everything.

I mean, another kid went out there in front of all of us and built this weird thing out of clay, and then there was like a pitter patter of clapping when he rolled it up and bowled it off stage before giving a bow. Maybe I was just worrying about my own performance. But, at that point, I was thinking if no one clapped for me, I was gonna literally curl up in ball and cry.

But when I finished my dance, they had clapped. Mom and Dad came through. And that was Mott needed right now.

"I mean, it has everything. I just got here, and I love it! It's kid friendly, the pictures are fabulous. All the characters are here. My mom and dad would buy one. Really, it's historical!"

I wasn't lying. I was in fact, truly mesmerized.

It won't ruin the story for me to go ahead and tell you I own two copies of her book now. One paperback and one hardcover.

Mott and Spock. Yeah. It's a circle with them. They inspired me then and still, they inspire me now.

The broadest smile came to Mott's face when I said as much and wouldn't you know it, I got one of those hugs that Vi enjoyed right off the bat. And it was some hug!

"Do you really mean it?" Mott asked.

"I do," I said. Feeling a bit like Dorothy telling the scarecrow that the wizard might give him a brain. I mean. I definitely wasn't in Kansas anymore.

"You know what, that means the world to me, darling." Mott pushed me back out to arm's length, "I would just love to meet the folks whose affection brought into this world such a creative soul as yours."

"Mott?" asked Vi.

"Yes, honey?"

Vi put the photo back onto the tabletop.

"What exactly was the act that Grandpa used to put on with Nan?"

Mott could remember it well.

Still, she could smell the district back when the circus arrived in town. The cages dragged in on trailers. In a single week her front yard would go from smelling of rain water and oil, to hay and funnel cakes.

She had been dating a vacuum cleaner salesman when she last saw Mr. Burchett's magic act. They were down in the standing area behind the metal barricades where they could be closest to the action. The area just beyond where the pigs ran circles around the center stage.

Mott had her hair pulled back and pinned with one of her custom wooden hair barrettes featuring a carved and painted daisy. As the Daisy vacuum cleaner was what her man, present beside her, was all about at the time.

She always had an artistic sales angle of her own to match whatever partners she found in love.

She was enjoying the Cracker Jacks that Larry, her boyfriend, had bought for her when Mr. Burchett took the stage, introduced by the Ringmaster as The Amazing Mr. Burchett and his bag of tricks.

Mr. Burchett was in a tuxedo complete with red bowtie and top hat. Tied at his waist was a burlap drawstring sack with candy cane striping. He gave the customary bow and really needed no introduction as many of the guests would have known him as the local owner of the Gem Shop. Regardless, he took the opportunity to drive up curiosity over his wares.

"Good evening, ladies, and gentlemen. I am Mr. Burchett. I own the local Gem Store here in the Art District. Be aware that while many of the amazing feats you have witnessed here are performed by professionals after thousands of hours of hard work and practice, what you are about to witness is the sum of a life of study."

With that Mr. Burchett untied the bag of tricks from his waist and dropped his top hat into it, then immediately turned it inside out showing only the tan burlap interior, revealing to the amazed audience that the bag was now completely empty. He noted, to the humor of many attended, that his head was now also quite cold.

But, as soon as everyone laughed and clapped, Mr. Burchett turned the bag right side out again to the candy cane exterior, reached an arm in to a fantastic depth. Far beyond the bottom of the bag, and when his arm withdrew, in it was his hat which he placed promptly atop his head.

The audience clapped. She remembered watching the bag waved limply around to prove it was indeed empty again. When Mr. Burchett removed his hat and circled it in the air to take his bow, the audience froze and pointed as a raven was nesting comfortably in his hair.

There was a theatrical exclamation in which Mr. Burchett had an elderly woman from the audience, some would recognize as Nan, come to the rescue and remove the bird, placing it gingerly back into the bag. The bag was then cinched shut with the drawstring, spun in a circle and then opened to the audience's amazement. Completely empty.

Mott had seen this act before on previous occasion but had never been selected as a participant until that fateful evening.

After much the same disappearing and reappearing performances, a small balancing act that seemed to defy gravity, and one time when Mr. Burchett had Nan pull a never-ending string of colored handkerchiefs from the sack, the grand finale finally arrived.

"We shall require the assistance of seven audience members who have objects of no great value that they can afford to lose in the name of art."

Larry elbowed Mott just as she had a cracker jack halfway to her mouth. "That's your cue, honey! Give him your barrette, it'll be great exposure for the Daisy."

One of the metal barricades was moved askew and seven audience members, including Mott, filed through and onto the stage for a closer look at the magic.

She recalled standing up there in the spotlight, her red dress tight around her hips and chest, and my lord, what she would do for a figure like that again! Each patron introduced themselves in turn and relinquished their personal item to Nan who came by with the microphone and collected.

An ink pen, a jelly bracelet, a half-dollar silver coin.

At that Mr. Burchett said, "Fear not patrons, you will have the opportunity to retrieve your goods at the end of the show."

A key ring (He didn't know what the keys went to anymore anyway, said the man), a plastic popcorn container, a ball cap, and Mott's daisy hair barrette, upon which she proudly said into the microphone, "Now, that's a custom piece. You'll get one with every Daisy Vacuum Cleaner. Remember, ya can't get really clean carpets without proper airflow."

This was a common theme in the Art District. Mott had grown up there and everything everywhere was an advertisement. Including, it turns out, Mr. Burchett's and Nan's Magic show.

The finale wasn't anything different than what had been going on throughout the whole ordeal except that each volunteer was allowed to look into the sack and see the collection of items resting at the bottom before the top was sealed shut and the bag given its customary spin.

The candy cane striped burlap sack was theatrically revealed once again to be empty and the act concluded with a pitch.

"Thank you, ladies, and gentlemen. Any items magicked away during this performance will be amazingly re-materialized in front of Nan's Thrift on your way out this afternoon. Don't worry. She won't make you buy them back from her as long as your nice.

Also, stop by the Gem Shop for magic tricks you can perform on your own."

"… and that was where and when that picture was taken," said Mott, pointing. "You can make out my barrette right there on the stand between the two."

Vi and I looked at each other.

Mott looked back and forth between us, that smile of hers ever-present.

"You two girls look like you've seen a ghost."

"How long have you lived here, Mott?" I asked.

Right then Mr. Bigglesworth jumped from Vi's lap and ran toward the archway where Spock and appeared. I thought of Dorothy's Toto jumping from the basket.

Mott said wistfully, "Well, as long as I can remember." Then she looked up with distant eyes at Spock.

Spock's tower of hair bounced about as he twirled his fingers at shoulder height pointing upwards. It was a little dance while Bigglesworth circled his feet.

He had apparently heard our conversation because he said without pause, "The District is a crab trap. Ever since I moved in, I've never been able to escape. It's like you can get in but you can't get out."

"Oh, don't get on with all that, Spock! He's fooling with you girls. Besides, if you don't want to get trapped, then don't take the bait." Mott sat back a final time.

Vi and I rose and then Spock said while lifting his bushy eyebrows at Mott, "But sometimes the bait is just smells so tasty."

Then he laughed a breathy sort of chuckle that was befitting of the comment.

Spock leaned down and grabbed the dog's leash and made a little narrow way for us to exit. He followed along behind us to the walk.

Vi and I got our bikes back up on two wheels before turning to wish him farewell.

"I would let you take it with you," Spock said. "But it needs to dry."

He was holding the leash lightly out to his right and stood with that top toothed permanent smile. Grey eyes flitting around like hummingbirds in a still cage.

We could see the easel.

On it was a picture of Vi, looking just like a walking lemonade stand, which accounted for all the yellows. Behind her was a pink unicorn looking over her shoulder.

We both hugged Spock at once. He bore it awkwardly and rigidly, almost seeming afraid of us both. When we finally let him free and got on our bicycles he said to us, "It'll be on the wall in the gallery if you every want to stop in and see."

Then we pedaled toward Vi's house and I couldn't help but notice that the sun was getting pretty low in the sky.

Chapter Thirteen

Well, we've crossed the hump, as Dad would say. If this were one of his fairy tales instead of something that really happened to my brother and I, and the cat I guess, Dad would be ready to start into the ending.

Begin wrapping it up because most of the story had been told.

Teen girl starts out part of a family with no real ties to robust culture. Loses her brother to said culture that she doesn't understand. Gets immersed in said culture and finds friends and happiness. Now must save said brother.

In the meantime, Mom and Dad were probably calling the National Guard because their kids were missing when they'd returned home from their date. Yet, I hadn't heard any sirens and home was only two miles from here, so that was mildly reassuring.

Honestly, if I had heard sirens on our way back down into the Gem Mine I don't think it would have changed anything. I really was lost in time right then. I was going to finish what I had started.

I had this terrible feeling that if I didn't finish, then I would be finished.

It was like Spock's painting or Mott's book. You don't just stop halfway with things or else some other weird universe is created where duty doesn't matter. Where self-respect has no meaning. And worse, where faith doesn't prevail. I didn't want to live in a weird world like that.

In fact, I was kind of liking the happy people over here in what I once called the ghetto.

My house may be a diamond in the rough, but out here, in the rough is where those diamonds are crafted. Out here, where people are under pressure. The smiles I've seen have taught me something.

You don't always need to know how to get out.

Maybe Spock was right. Sometimes you just have to take the bait.

Nan's Shop was definitely the king of all crab traps if there ever was one.

But I was going to spring it.

Chapter Fourteen

What was it about that blouse that was making Nan feel uneasy?

After the cute, yet awkward girl in the pink unicorn outfit had left, Nan had tagged the returned item, thought of writing one ninety-nine and instead wrote two ninety-nine on the little red price tag, then made her way around the counter to rack the item.

She saw the girls shifting silhouette outside of the stained-glass window. Still, she felt uneasy for some reason. That had been the only customer all day.

The tired old woman flipped through the rack of used items. Sliding hangers over one by one. Did she think she saw that girl making her way around back?

Flip, flip. That's strange, Nan thought scratching her nose. What happened to the little red onesie she had just placed here this morning?

Nan's good eye went to its corner in sharp consternation. She snarled a little.

Suppose she was getting a bit crabby in her old age?

It didn't take long for Vi and I to undo the tackle from the lift down in the cave of wonders. Ms. Burchett gave us no trouble at all.

In fact, Vi told her everything!

She sat there on the stool in her shop with her work boot propped up on the counter and her chin resting on her knuckles listening as Vi railed off the entire plan.

"We're probably gonna use the wagon—"

"Uh huh," Ms. Burchett would say nodding and blowing a big pink bubble.

"—Then we're gonna sneak Tanner down into her basement, which she thinks is a giant crab trap."

"I see," Ms. Burchett said beginning to file her fingernails. "And are you going to need any help?"

I almost couldn't stand the absolute disregard to reason that Ms. Burchett was allowing her daughter, but I had to admit, I was totally and completely jealous!

I almost interrupted, but Vi was on a roll like a mad scientist reeling off his evil plans.

"I'm pretty sure if she finds the pop-up point she'll find her brother and I can hoist her out."

When Vi had finished, her mother was looking at her expectantly.

Vi went on cautiously, "—and, we will be home before dinner?"

"Okay," said Ms. Burchett, but I will be checking with Nan this evening if I don't get a complete report from the two of you. "And you know, Vi, I still don't want you past where the sidewalk ends."

I thought of a poem book my dad used to read me at bedtime and all-of-a-sudden considered Hungry Mongry a terribly scary tale.

Nan was going to tidy up in the back when she thought she saw that unicorn girl staring in through a basement window.

She may have gone out to see what the problem was had not that wretched cat streaked across the basement and sent a pile of aluminum hub caps rolling wildly around.

Where had that cat come from, she wondered. This was the second time she'd seen it this week.

Nan's perch had been acting up since the circus left town two years back. Well, it could have to do with that, or the giant pile of socks that rested atop the quartz catch.

Nan never considered herself an evil witch. Who on Earth would think of themselves in that regard? Though, if the patrons of the Art District found out that all of their single socks were due to the cavern beneath Nan's Curiosities, she might be labeled as such.

But what's life without mystery? And she did feel that she had become a bit sour since Mr. Burchett passed. Life just wasn't as magical without the crowds and without, well, the magic.

She gave the old cavern one more look after tidying up downstairs. Considered taking the flashlight down to see if any new items had wiggled their way through the mess, but reconsidered.

Then she made her way back through the beads and into the hall between the front of the shop and the rear. To her right there was a staircase that led up to the loft where she could put on a spot of tea.

She paused by the beads leading to the register, heard no bells jingle to indicate another customer, and began the climb up to her personal apartment.

Upstairs, Nan could look out of her black little window over the district and remember the days when the Lumpin Circus brought in droves of children and families.

While she waited for the kettle to start whistling, she thought of how the numbers had dwindled with each passing year. Like Mr. Burchett's collection of shoes had dwindled.

She cursed the man for being so spot on with his own disappearance. A magician through and through.

The pot began to sing. A thin line of steam blowing from the lips of the silver little ditty. Only when the lid began to rattle did she find her way from the window and to the stove to pour a cup.

"Well, the sun's getting low," she thought wearily. "Guess we should close up shop." She peeked down through the banister at the stuffed raven that hung over the shop's front door. As usual, the old raven just sat atop its perch silently. Another piece of magic lost to time.

The boards creaked on the last two steps before the landing and Nan moved the beads aside, stepping out into her shop.

Had she seen a flash of orange and white fur?

She wouldn't curse it. Maybe a little life is coming back to her after all?

What really was on her mind was the blouse that girl had returned. Hadn't she just sold that garment not two days prior?

Something was itching her right under the old fold that used to tell her that she'd been missing something important. You got folds like that in the neder regions especially when you'd been around as long as she.

Could it be?

Could that old bag of tricks have still had some magic left in it?

She stopped at the roundy gondola of second-hand shirts and blouses lifting a red tag to the stained-glass light.

Well, she thought. It'd likely take more than a unicorn to bring the old Magic back to us…

Then Nan saw something through the stained glass that gave her pause.

That darned girl! Standing out there on the porch with her bicycle. That confounded girl in the unicorn costume! The one who'd been snooping around.

Nan wasn't sour. Nan was just quickly getting set in her ways. And when it was time to close up shop, that was that. It doesn't take long to grow old, thought Nan, as she marched out beneath the old raven to the front door.

One day you're inviting and fun, the next you're an old crow running off the teenagers before sunset so as your tea doesn't turn cold.

She opened the front door, and saw—

The girl's unicorn onesie propped up on a broom stick sitting atop her bicycle by the stairs.

Nan looked right and left feeling like some cruel trick was about to be played on her. But the lot was empty save the odd scarecrow. She closed the door and shot the bolt. Then she pulled her old cloak taught around her.

"Just what the heck is that Dear girl up to?"

Chapter Fifteen

Under the privacy of Vi's basement, I had taken off my Unicorn Onesie and replaced it with something a bit more functional. My favorite jeans of course! The ones I had traded for the blouse Mom had picked out for me.

Honestly, that was a relief, as they'd worked their way into a bunch at my right ankle and I was walking around like I had a troll foot or something.

At present, the backside of said blue jeans was sliding along the moldy rock wall of the well behind Mrs. Partridge's with my rear firmly inside. My sneaker was literally in front of my face and I wondered if it wasn't time to put the whole obsession with pink thing behind me.

Vi and I had secured the tackle and she was feeding the rope out over the wench little by little. It had a locking mechanism that clicked every time I went down a little bit.

"How's it coming?" came Vi's voice from above. I could see her shadow peek over the edge of the stone well.

"Well, enough." No pun intended, I thought. What can I say? Dad jokes.

About now, Spock should have wheeled our 'sculpture' up and parked it in front of Nan's.

Sculpture was a longshot. But look who we were talking to. I'm pretty sure if we'd have told him it was a distraction, it would have made no difference.

The plywood which covered the well had been the worst part thus far, at least until *this*. Vi and I just had to push it off the well and most if it simply disintegrated when it hit the sand on the other side with a THWUMP.

Everything was so dry and old.

The little decorative bucket was no trouble, it clipped right off but Vi said that the carabiner wasn't trusty, so she used all of the stuff we wheeled over in the wagon.

The big clip, pulleys, and our own rope, plus the winch catch with the handle. All attached to the eye bolt hanging from the well's cute little roof. The whole thing might fall in, yes. But I was pretty confident in my ability to hold myself up against the walls.

Looking back, that was stupid.

I was in no kind of shape to be wedged into that well the way I was!

I was certain that my athletic ability wasn't keeping any strain off of the pulley system as I descended.

The progress was slow but I was managing the only way I could.

I would slide my back sneaker down, which I was practically sitting on, then I would walk my front foot down an inch or so. Then the whole contraption would make a CLICK, and I could feel the rope vibrate.

My left hand was on the wall in front of me and my right hand on the rope. I was looking up, but Vi had gone back to holding tension and some dust fell into my eye.

I looked down and tried shaking it free by blinking. My little plastic flashlight joby was in my left hip pocket and flashed in my eyes when I palmed at the dust.

CLICK!

My back foot lost traction and I slipped down a notch, but the winch held and I struggled to get my feet back firm in their grips. I had to let go of the wall with my left hand to try and catch the flashlight that had shifted out to the edge of its handle.

I was too late.

Between letting the noisy rope hold all of my weight and letting the flashlight fall, it was a no brainer. I could do nothing but watch it do cartwheels down into the dark.

I let out a breath as it made its descending turns. A yellow lighthouse dropping into the abyss. White as it hit my eyes, then gray stone wall, yellowed darkness, grey stone wall. White, grey, yellow, grey. White, grey...

And just as it reached the bottom, on its final two turns, I could make out the dingy whiteness of the floor fifty feet below. Then the light was gone, obliterated on what I now realized was the shiny quartz like I had seen in the well at Vi's.

For a moment I was in the dark.

Hanging there at the spot where the light coming from above was of no help in seeing what was around me.

Below me however, I could see the dim glow of artificial light pouring in over part of the base.

Vi was feeding out more rope, and I was frantically sliding down inch by inch at the end of its tension, scared that I no longer had the strength to climb up. No, I knew I didn't have the strength to climb up and now I doubted I could make it down.

I was going to have to let the rope take the whole weight of me. Again, I looked up, hoping to see Vi, this time shielding my eyes with my worthless left hand.

The was a double knot in the rope squeezed between my thighs, which I could easily cling to, but I could feel the tremble of the rope and then a shift in the pulley again.

"Ah!" I slipped again. Just another two inches before I wedged myself for a final effort between the walls.

Then I yelped out, "Aha ha!" Probably the most nervous laugh anyone had ever heard and now my arms and legs were shaking uncontrollably.

VI poked her head back over the edge.

"You okay, Tanner?"

I wasn't.

I was slipping and was about to say as much when I took a deep breath and just decided to trust the tackle. I squeezed my thighs and hugged the rope.

CLICK!

It held!

My gosh it held. And it felt terrible hanging there out in space on that knot.

"I've got you!" came Vi from above.

I could feel the rope pull a little then CLICK!

I dropped a whole foot. Instinctively I reached out my left hand and tried scissoring my feet again. But it would have been no use. I clung back to the rope and felt the wall of the well brush my hip as I swayed a little under the motion.

I was hanging still again.

"I got it!" yelled Vi again.

Then another foot drop and this time CLICK, CLICK! I just squeezed the rope and shut my eyes. But something was wrong. Now the wall was right up against me and I felt wood pieces rain around me.

Something had shifted. I shielded my eyes again and tried looking up.

CLICK! CLICK! CLICK!

This time the drop was two feet and I was resting against the other wall.

I squinted up through the dark and could see the tackle was askew. The eye-bolt was working its way out of the old wooden roof.

"I got thi—" Vi's voice was cut off by a CLICK, CLICK, CLICK, CLICK, CLICK.

My belly went straight to my throat as the tackle came free and I tried for my life to cling to the walls of the dark well.

Back in the Banyan

Kristen was lying in the dirt on her stomach with her ear turned to the upturned face of Death. Her grip on her fluffy bunny pen was strangling. Her arms were crossed under her chin and Death could sense her obvious tension.

When she realized the story had paused, she turned her face to Death and saw him looking up. He was still holding the shoe, only now in both hands and his scythe was again camouflaged against the wooden pile of trinkets.

"What's wrong?" she asked pointedly.

"Tanner does not die here," He said hollowly.

"What?!"

"I'm only telling you because you look like you're concerned."

Kristen loosened her grip and tried to look less rigid.

"I'm just concerned about the time is all," she said.

"I see," said Death. "I told you already, Chronos will be fine."

She shifted her position and pulled her t-shirt tight again, removing the wrinkles that had started forming semi-permanent fissures in her skin from lying there so long.

"You know what I mean! I have to make it to the school after closing bell or the boys will come looking for me."

"Then I guess we should get on with it?"

"Please," she said.

Say what you will about instinct, Tanner continued.

I had a friend once in track who swore she could run faster than I could if someone were chasing her and trying to kill her with a knife or something. I just thought she was making excuses because she was lazy.

My instinct was to save myself by not falling down that well. Because, *that* was going to kill me.

Yes, well, that did not save me. If you can't grab anything, you can't grab anything.

Honestly, after I initially knew I was falling, my head just went all swimmy. The fact that I'm standing here today tells you I survived and looking back I might say something like, I was just wishing I would wake up.

But, the only truth I know, is that no instinct whatsoever saved my life in those horrifying seconds.

No instinct at all. It was socks that did that.

The pile of socks that I landed on weren't as you would expect. Of course, there were gym socks, the long tube-like ones with two stripes at top. There were frilly socks. Wool socks. Heck, it was a hay stack of socks of all sorts. But none of them smelled bad as far as I could tell.

In fact, they all smelled quiet nice. My landing wasn't exactly how the bounty soft teddy bear falls into the pile of laundry, but I was gonna take what I could get.

I hit it like a… Well, I don't exactly know, because my eyes were shut. I just kinda skidded down the side of the pile and out onto the floor of Mrs. Partridge's little cavern.

The rope coiled down beside me shortly after. Followed by Vi's echoing pleas. "I'm sorry, Tanner!"

There would now be no escaping that way. Regardless, I climbed back up the pile of laundry and ducked my head under the ledge of the hole I had fallen through. I could only see a circle of light with the faintest shroud of shadow up there.

"Good luck, Tanner!"

I thought better than to yell back, and then as if in an answer of confidence I watched the light get blotted out from above. It was what was left of the plywood being slid back in place.

I was on my own.

I would argue that most of the socks in that pile were loners. By the way they smelled so fresh when I slid back down, I would also argue that they went into someone's dryer but never made it back out.

But the fact was, I didn't die on a rocky outcropping of quartz. It was just that most of the socks were white.

Easy mistake to make when you're hanging fifty feet above probable doom.

The small tunnel I was in was dry. Knitted rugs hung along the walls while the floor was a patchwork of AstroTurf. It was light enough, as not more than thirty feet away I could see the opening into Mrs. Partridge's basement.

Beads were hanging along the edges of where the cavern made a threshold with the shop's framework.

I grabbed up my plastic flashlight that looked to have survived the fall but was out like, well, a light. I shook it and it gave no sign of life. Just some beady little noise like there was plastic pieces loose inside of the handle.

Toast, I guessed.

It was bright enough to see at least, and for the most part was a bit like the cave of wonders, except along the edges of the walk-up weren't crystals and jewels. But piles of other articles of clothing. Sorted out into their basic groups.

Wooden trilithons stood every ten feet or so, you know those railroad ties for support, though the cavern surely was in no danger of collapse. They were old dark wood and made me think a minecart wouldn't have been out of place, though it would have nowhere to go.

I walked by a pile of pajamas on the left and shorts on the right.

Next up were trousers across from a spattering of winter coats. And then a bulging mess of unmentionables.

That, moved.

"Gabe?!"

My baby brother was exactly where Mom would have loved to find him. Rolling about in the questionable underwear!

He was up on his feet and running like I had never seen before. Then to my heart's relief he was in my hands and I was smothering him with kisses.

In his hand was one of the socks I had made a three-point-shot with.

Maybe some of those socks were dirties.

"You stinker!" I took the sock from him and stuffed it in the pocket of my jeans. "Now, let's get out of here."

"Cool," he said. And that time, he definitely said cool.

Poor guy was growing up.

Maybe we both were.

Chapter Sixteen

I finally had my baby brother. There would be no denying it when we ran into Mrs. Partridge. Right then, I could imagine that I was back at home again. It was only a short walk away.

No way I was putting him on my bike. No Siree, when I was out that door I was running as fast as I could carry the guy! I bet Mom and Dad were home already and freaking out to high heaven. If they saw us coming up the road everything might just be okay.

I could say we were out for a walk, that someone had taken the bike off the porch. Yeah, that would work!

Then everything would be back to normal.

Normal. What a thought.

The floor of Nan's cache, as Vi had called it, had a slight slope, reminding me of Vi's unfinished basement. But this was finished, of course.

Gabe was behaving. I had his hand and we were in the middle of the basement looking up at the beads that I had seen Mrs. Partridge come through earlier that day. Then, I remembered the half-buried window I had been looking through.

I turned and looked up to it.

Vi was there! Her glasses and red hair brilliant, and she was waving. Gabe lifted his hand and blurted out, "Tanner."

I got him and pulled him close behind the pile of wooden crafts and tried hushing him, though I was just so proud of him for saying my name.

Our backs were against the pile, the wooden rocking horse poking out above us.

I could see Vi's expression up there. One of excitement.

She was probably relieved that I was alive!

But then, I saw her do something I was all too familiar with.

There was a brief flash of horror in Vi's face and she pushed off of the little window with both hands and disappeared.

She thought she had been spotted, and I knew it because, behind us, I heard the beads swish as Mrs. Partridge entered the basement.

The wicked witch was in the room.

I felt like Grettle trying to save Hansel, but there wasn't an oven to push her into. I wasn't sure what I was going to do. Couldn't she just kill me if she caught us trespassing?

Our snoopy old neighbor had always threatened as much and Dad had always told us to stay off his property because it was his right to do as he pleased there.

Mrs. Partridge may have seen Vi in the window because she said something indiscernible to herself. Whatever it was she said, I heard something that sounded to me like, "Where is that Hansel?"

I was sweating. Gabe was kicking his soft feet playfully and gnawing on his knuckle. Still wrapped up safely in his own onesie. And still dry!

Had I been eaten by a hamper, the first thing I would have had to do was change my pants!

I had heard the beads close behind the witch but hadn't heard any footsteps. I dared a look around the side of the pile.

Nothing.

I scooped up Gabe and went for the bead doorway. There were only three steps up to it, but I didn't see what I expected when I pushed our heads through.

We were in a hallway that led to a door which was sitting ajar and across from us was another beaded entrance. I knew, as soon as I saw the pattern that it was the way to the shop and our freedom.

How I could have mistaken this rodeo styled checked pattern for the plastic bones and beads I won't ever know, but I had not expected as much.

Regardless, I went through.

There was no way to do it quietly. Beads ponged and ticked together like that darn rain stick I had first played with on my first visit. It was darker in there now.

I had to reach up and grab Gabe's hand as he tried to keep a bone for himself.

Among all the swishing I came to the absolute realization that I was going to have to confront Mrs. Partridge like a real human being and was struck so totally dumb by it that I didn't realize the Raven over the doorframe had come to life.

It squawked at us when we went to duck beneath the entryway. Alarmed, I tucked Gabe back away toward the counter. That's when Mrs. Partridge showed up.

"I knew it was, you!" The witch croaked, splashing through the beads behind the counter. "As soon as I realized it was your mother I had sold that Hamper to! It's working again, isn't it?"

The old woman was mad!

The crow squawked from its perch above the door and nipped at the wiry mess of hair on her head while she closed in on us.

There was nowhere to retreat to besides towards the section of second-hand clothes and there was no way out. We were trapped.

The raven cawed when Mrs. Partridge absently brushed its beak from her hair. Gabe started squalling.

Mrs. Partridge, her teeth, her bob hair, her one long fingernail and hands seemed to all be reaching for me at once, when I tripped backwards. And that was the last and largest thing I saw before Pixie jumped from the countertop behind her right into my arms.

The three of us, Me, Gabe, and Pixie all tumbled backward into the round gondola of clothing.

I can remember the look on Mrs. Partridge's face. Okay, her real name is Nan.

To me, as a thirteen-year-old girl, the look was one of total terror. Which scared me more than a look of total hatred would have. And now, that I know what I know, I can see why she was giving me that look as I fell into the center of that magical gondola.

At the time, I was a teenager, with her hands full of a baby brother and a cat to boot. But still I had keen eyes.

While I was falling through, right into that mess of clothing, I got a glimpse of the blouse Mom had bought for me wrinkle by on its hanger before cool air enveloped us and a cracking sound left us all spilling out onto my bedroom floor.

My bedroom floor!

Right in front of me was that red onesie on the floor and beyond that the broken hamper, white wicker cracked open, yet the liner was still in tact. I didn't stop to think.

Now imagine the old witch's reaction on the other side of that perch, or portal or whatever, when I reached back into the broken hamper and pulled my blouse out like Mr. Burchett may have done from his magic bag all those years ago!

Good as new, too. With a price tag still on it that read two ninety-nine.

But, then something happened that I didn't expect.

That old grubby hand of hers with the one long fingernail came through the bottom of the hamper's lining, grabbing around for something to gain purchase.

I scooched back on my butt pressing Gabe back with my arm and we watched as it quickly felt along the floor by the bin. I kicked the red onesie that I had technically stolen, over to the dancing fingers.

The old woman's agile fingers, and long nail, seized the onesie then grabbed the knot on the burlap sack and yanked it all right in on itself.

For a brief moment, I could see the outside of the hamper's liner right before it disappeared in on itself and was gone, leaving only the splintered wicker shell and debris on the bedroom floor.

Unmistakably, the liner of the old hamper had pink and white stripes. A candy cane design, faded with time.

The sun was shining, as the curtains were still thrown and pixie went right to her spot on the bed. Gabe was on his feet. We were both by his crib, me finally flabbergasted at what on Earth just occurred.

"Tanner!" he piped in my ear, and that just sealed it. We were back from the Art District!

I hugged him into my lap and tickled him, causing a bit more of a commotion than I felt up to, really.

And then, the bedroom door crashed open.

Chapter Seventeen

Dad burst in with Mom over his shoulder. He hadn't let go of the door handle before Mom's smile faded.

"Tanner?" she scolded, "What on Earth?"

I thought that was putting it mildly.

Dad was doing his normal thing trying to look mad, but wasn't doing a very good job of it.

I looked around, then pulled Gabe in for another hug.

Dad gave Mom a look that said to let it go. Then, Mom ducked under his arm and came full into the room, righting the hamper best it could be righted. It was hopelessly destroyed.

"Well, you could have just said you didn't like it," Mom said.

I was entirely unsure what was going on. There were no police involved so that was a good sign so far.

"The cat," I started to offer, then Gabe said, "Tanner!"

Dad started laughing. Mom chuckled a little and picked up my little guy, "You see?" Mom said. "You're not gonna be able to get away with things so easily anymore."

Then she gave him a nosey and said, "Say it again, Gabe. Is that Tanner?"

Dad was watching me as she snuggled the little dude and I was getting up on my feet. His look was a mix of humility and encouragement.

That was the way he looked at me sometimes. A look that said, "Things are going well. Let's keep it going."

So, I did.

I picked up a few flecks of white paint and wicker wood, tossing them in the broken hamper. Then I held out the blouse to Mom.

"Would you mind washing this? It smells like moth balls."

She put Gabe down and took it from my hand. Then she dropped her hand to her side.

"So, you're not going to ask?"

"Ask what?" I said. Literally, I was still wondering if the dampness on my butt was from the well or if I had maybe crapped my pants.

"Tanner!" Mom said, growing irritated. Then, "About the movie? Why we're home so late?"

I was definitely back to reality!

"Oh." I said, probably looking like I was high as a kite.

But that's the advantage of being a little dim. No one ever really knows if your really just that stupid or not. Hey, I mean it had worked on Mrs. Partridge.

"What did you guys go see?" I asked.

Would you freakin' believe it? It was one of those Stephen King flicks. A remake of IT or something. And what my Dad said next was just plain irony at its best.

"They don't need to know the details. The kids are too young to handle movies like that." He shook his head in disgust, then said, "But we did go out to Dinner."

"Chili's?"

"Nah, Friday's," he said.

I gave him a good ole 'Go-team' bicep curl and said, "Dad's dinner and a movie special, eh?"

Mom was the one rolling her eyes.

That was a change.

As she ducked back beneath Dad's arm with my blouse and headed toward the washer and dryer, I saw her eyeing something between her fingers.

The red price tag that now read two ninety-nine.

Back on Mrs. Partridge's side of the district. Nan was holding the red onesie and the candy cane bag of tricks while laughing hysterically.

To a frightened teenage girl, it may have seemed like maniacal laughter.

But, to a tired old lady, it was one of hope and joy.

The magic had finally returned!

And her old friend, the raven, laughed with her.

There wasn't much of a mess to clean up as far as my room was concerned.

I felt really bad about lying about the bike. Or at least pretending that I didn't know anything. That blew over.

The real mess was the following month when school let out for winter.

I had been nervous for weeks that Mom may have returned to Nan's Curiosities and found my bike, or my unicorn outfit on a shelf, and started a whole investigation, but it never happened.

It was when Dad showed me three tickets to the Lumpin Family Circus that things got really interesting. It was gonna be a first timer for Gabe. But I couldn't stop thinking about who I might see over there in the Art District during our visit.

To my pleasant surprise, we walked.

We went on a Wednesday night when Mom was working at the church.

It had been in town for a few days, and I had already seen the tents and commotion from the school bus. It actually looked fun.

From the bus windows, I had seen kids and parents packed into the little district. I could imagine Vi helping out with mining behind her mom's house and Spock painting caricatures of couples with their pets.

I knew something for sure that I hadn't been so sure of a whole year ago. The Art District was definitely not the ghetto.

Right before Dad, Gabe, and I crossed Tamiami trail we came across a huddle of homeless men and women on the corner. That kind of thing is common being only a few blocks from the Salvation Army.

It's Florida so it doesn't get that cold down here, but there was a slight nip to the air and this group had a crocheted blanket big enough to cover them all up together. It was the same colors as the beads in Nan's basement. All Mexican-cowboy designed.

Dad held out a twenty and said, "Who can divvy this up between you all?"

One skinny black man's hand darted out from under the blanket like an arrow.

"I can do that, Sir. I'm good at math! That's, let's see," he was doing some quick calculation on his fingers. "That's three dollars for each of them and two for me," he said and then took the bill from my dad.

Just for a moment, I thought the guy looked fishy. The old me might have believed he was going to keep it all for himself, but today I saw a fellow. Maybe it was a person in need who had just maybe gotten such a quilt from a shop with an overabundance of unneeded things, but still, a fellow!

The traffic got a break in it, and Dad picked up Gabe then rushed us across the main road.

Along the way, we passed by jugglers, bubble blowers, fire-eaters. There was a hotdog cart, manned by a clown.

The crowd wasn't as large as a State Fair or anything, but there were lots of families. When we came to the crossroads, Dad put Gabe down and let him walk with me holding his hand. A cheap temporary sign was pushed into the dirt by the real post which had an arrow and the logo for the circus pointing toward Mott's place.

No sign would have been needed, really. You couldn't miss the giant tent and orange cones. Plus, there were temporary yellow ropes cordoning off the lot across from Spock and Mott's.

I showed Gabe the hop scotch on the sidewalk and had him join me in a quick game along the way. Most people didn't even notice it was there!

Spock and Mott's place was kind of dull in contrast to the street noise. But I saw a glow under the lanai and knew that the gallery would be open to the public when we were done.

Also, I had to point out the sculpture in the front yard as if I had never seen it before. Dad gave me an evil eye when I slapped one of the hub caps that were dangling off and made it CLANG against the others.

"What d'ya think you own the place?" that look said.

I thought of when I'd first met Vi behind Mrs. Partridge's place, when she'd wheeled up in her yellow visor asking if I was a unicorn or wasn't I. Then I understood what it meant to be part of something, and I thought, 'Yeah. I kinda do think I own the place.'

Chapter Eighteen

I wasn't Gabe's age when I first went to the circus. But I kinda wish I had been.

I could see the wonder in the reflections of his eyes the whole time.

Little do we ever think of the effort, the art, the manpower, and the love that is put into something like a little hometown family circus. But I felt it the time that Dad and I took Gabe.

People were doing things just to do them. Just to see the smile on someone's face.

A clown was stealing a man's popcorn and throwing it into the air, intentionally failing to catch it in his mouth.

Kids were laughing.

There were all of the classics. The lions and elephants. Then, a teeterboard act.

Five acrobats launched from a seesaw onto the shoulders of one after another, until the whole family stood like a totem pole. The final member, the youngest and smallest, did a double back flip off the end of the teeterboard and landed upright on the very top of the four others.

Then they tipped forward like a tree falling and all of them rolled agilely away unharmed.

It was magnificent!

I even got a snapshot of Gabe with a piece of popcorn halfway to his mouth in awe.

The three of us were down in front, behind the metal barriers where the pigs were running circles around the center stage, when Ms. Burchett was announced as, The Magical Ms. Burchett and her bag of tricks.

To my delight, Vi's mom took center stage. At her waist was a candy cane burlap sack. She had a top hat, which looked oddly out of place since she still wore her leather tool belt.

Dressed in a top half tuxedo and a bottom half Gemmine-approved skirt and boots, she did a little jig, like Spock may have taught her, and took the top hat off her head in a salute.

She was looking directly at me when she started.

But really, it wasn't me she was looking at, it was Vi who had snuck up beside me.

"Tanner?"

"Oh, my gosh! Vi!"

She hugged me before I could hug her.

"I thought you were dead!" she screamed at a whisper, trying not to interrupt her mom's performance.

It was pretty noisy anyhow, but we were right up front where everyone could see us.

I gave Dad a minor guilty look, but he didn't seem to think anything of it.

"And, this is Gabe!" Vi pressed her lips against his cheek even though he was looking straight out toward the stage where Ms. Burchett had already put the top hat in the bag and was making it disappear.

Then, Dad picked him up to see better and Vi pulled me down to my knees where it actually seemed a little more private.

"Can you believe it?" Vi asked.

"No," I shook my head, eyes wide. "I mean yes. Your mom's really putting on your grandpa's old act?"

Vi smiled, "Third time this week." Then she took a huge breath and said, "Man! After you didn't show up for dinner, Mom went down to Nan's to raise the roof."

I was looking right through those glasses at her, still a little dumbstruck that I was with her again.

"After it turned dark, I couldn't figure what happened to Mom, so I closed up shop myself and strolled out to Nan's with the hit-a-person flashlight. You know, the one your Mom calls it—"

"Yes, yes." I said, taking a quick glance out to the performance over Gabe's shoulder as not to miss anything. But she pulled me back down just as I caught sight of the raven on Ms. Burchett's head. "Well, spit it out!" I urged, not wanting to miss more of the act.

"Would you believe it? Spock and Mott, Mom, and Nan were in there with the strobe lights going and the fog machine rolling, shaking rain sticks. Going all kinds of crazy!"

Vi had a look that said she couldn't believe what she was saying but went on, "I honestly didn't know what to make of it!"

I was trying to picture it.

That old sour witch, happy-go-lucky Mott and Spock, and cool Ms. Burchett all in that Crab Trap together and what they would have been doing.

I was dying to watch the performance, but Vi wouldn't let me up.

"It was a party, Tanner. They were in there reminiscing about Mr. Burchett and how he used to magic things away to Nan's shop. Mott had her book in there showing it to Nan.

Turns out Nan had lost hope after Mr. Burchett died and that old burlap sack just went on depressing Granny Nan more and more each year."

I looked to my right in thought and saw the light coming through Dads trousers and changing all kinds of colors. Then looked up along the metal barriers and saw the pigs beginning to do their rounds.

I looked at Vi, who was smiling, and I almost wanted to put my thumb in my mouth and bite down hard just to be sure I was awake. But I didn't have to.

"Your Mom's got it up there? Doesn't she?" I said.

Vi looked me straight in the eye and nodded.

That one moment in my life, it will always be the sweetest.

Nah. We haven't reached the very end just yet. But that moment was the best part of my story, as far as it went, because I have heard that a beautiful thing like that can never be captured in words.

But I like to think I've done a pretty good job of it. You were probably wondering just how I knew Nan's point of view when I started writing about what she was going through earlier.

Well, truth is, back then, I wouldn't have. That took time over the next couple years, up to now, to really get to know Granny Nan.

Turns out it's not very nice to call someone Mrs. Partridge just because their hair makes you think of a perched bird. Or to judge someone because of their teeth. But now I know better and Gabe may grow up and not be so prejudiced as I.

Though I still will write scary stories that will threaten to make innocent little guys like him play the victim. And that would be thanks to Dad.

But, I do it out of love for the guy. Hey, it pays the bills.

Least that what Dad says it will do if I keep this up for thirty years!

And all I have is time.

So, here goes nothing, starting with what happened that day at the circus, because it just wouldn't be right to leave you hanging on here wondering about how my relationship with Mom turned out, and if and where you can buy one of Mott's books… or mine.

So, keep reading.

And that, my friends, is an invitation as well as the best piece of advice I have given or received.

So, we all watched Ms. Burchett's mockup of Mr. Burchett's performance with the magic burlap sack, pretty much copied and pasted. With only one little difference.

Gabe and I were picked to come up on stage with the other six volunteers. We were placed at the end of the line as a Grand finale, of course.

Nan came up and collected the items from the six volunteers, her milky eye sizing up each one as she went. She then placed them into Ms. Burchett's bag.

Then, as Ms. Burchett was walking along and showing each person in line that the contents were still there, Nan leaned into my ear and said, "It seems that there's no magic without children around. Your little brother seemed to find a way to turn things around, Dear."

She no longer seemed a scary old witch.

Ms. Burchett stopped in front of Gabe and I. She asked me if Vi had filled me in. I nodded and looked at Gabe.

She placed the burlap candy-cane sack on the floor and knelt beside it, opening the mouth of it and tilting it in a way Gabe could look inside.

Then, wouldn't you know it? I let go of Gabe's hand and he crawled right in.

Nan put her hand on my shoulder and Ms. Burchett gave me a kind little wink before closing the sack. I looked out and saw Dad appearing a little nervous. Meanwhile, Vi who stood nearby him was clapping with giddiness.

Then, Ms. Burchett closed the sack and said, "Abracadam!"

She lifted off her top hat in salute and stood up with the sack in one hand, showing that it weighed nothing.

She then turned the bag inside out revealing that all had totally disappeared.

The crowd went wild.

The metal barriers were open again and I returned to Dad's side as Nan was closing the act, of course, punctuating every line with Dear.

Dad obviously wasn't listening because Nan had already answered his coming question. As soon as I was close enough, he blurted out, "What on Earth happened to Gabe?"

"Don't worry, Dad," I said. "I have a feeling I know exactly where he is."

The circus was doing the curtain call so Vi, Dad and I escaped early to Nan's shop. Apparently Vi was no longer forbidden to cross where the sidewalk ends.

I was slightly disappointed in not getting to take Dad by Spock and Mott's studio, but I didn't think he would be down for a detour before making sure Gabe was safe.

To my surprise, Mott was standing out front of Nan's Curiosities by a wooden folding table holding Gabe's hand. Her eyes and smile brightened even more than usual when she saw us approaching. The closer we got, the more it was obvious that the spread on the table included all of the items from the act.

Also on the table were multiple copies of Mott's book in sparkling new condition.

"Eew we!" hollered Mott, "You beautiful child! What a blessing to see you again!"

Dad got down on his knee and hiked a happy Gabe up into his arms. Gabe had seemed to acquire a new stuffed animal.

"Friend of yours?" Dad asked me.

I tried not to look too guilty and said, "It's a long story."

"A story," Vi interrupter, "That you can read all about in Mott's new book."

"Can we buy one, Dad?"

Before he could even object, the front door to Nan's came open and Spock came dancing down the front steps. He was shaking one of the rain sticks I had first encountered on my adventure.

He did a little twirl as he got near and then a theatrical bow. Making his top hat of hair bounce before being swept up in a shimmy with the wind.

"This is for you, kiddo," he said, handing me the stick. "Nan said to make sure you got it if she was still closing up at the circus."

Dad watched this exchange with more than a little confusion. Then he said something that would have made Mom proud.

"Well, I guess we have to buy *something.*"

You can probably guess that was when I got my first copy of Mott's manuscript.

Shortly after, we headed home but not before Vi handed us a voucher for the gem mine and asked if we would bring Gabe back to find some jewels.

"I think he would like that," Dad said.

Some people think that my story is a bunch of bull crap. Even when I show them the ending of Mott's book that tells all about two little girls and a baby boy that brought magic back to the Art District.

It's amazing really. Yes, that Magic returned. But also amazing that people still don't believe me, even when I show them the painting on the final page featuring Vi and I. A photocopy of the painting hanging on the wall in Mott and Spock's studio. It's a bit abstract, of course, but so was our adventure.

Gabe and I are now regular customers at the Gem Mine. He loves sifting for gems and has quite the collection. I enjoy writing. Who knows, maybe one day some of my stuff will be on sale after the Lumpin Family Circus.

Mom went with us to the Circus this last year. She even asked me to help her pick out her outfit. I noticed she had even laid out a thong!

These, days my clothes make it all the way to the laundry room. I prefer it that way, because every time I walk to the washer, I get to count the faces of my family.

I'm almost eighteen now and might be moving out soon. I guess this kind of happiness can't last forever, ya know. But that's okay. There aren't many girls who can say that they ever ended up with a double happy ending.

TIME GOES ON

Kristen had been lying there trying to envision the Village of the Arts in its former glory. She was considering whether or not a magic show like that here and now would tear anyone away from their virtual reality or televisions long enough to enjoy it.

Her crew still liked playing paintball, so she thought it might be possible. But paintball was a skill they could carry with them when they were allowed to participate in the games. In the outside world, most of the younger crowd were involved in the high-stakes entertainment franchise catering to the super rich.

Coordination and physical conditioning was important to nurture before getting a visa. Else, you start out spoiled and rely totally on magic for everything, and no one wanted to become a witch or a wizard. Magic-types were all known to be terribly self indulgent! And the only way to rise up in the ranks of those jobs was to outlive one of your superiors.

She was biting down on the bunny's tail, pen in hand, staring at her journal. She had nearly filled up the entire thing.

She thought of what simple magic it was that had brought the crowds back here.

"In a way," she said to Death, who had lifted the hamper's lid and was positioned to drop the dilapidated shoe inside. He paused and looked at her.

She continued. "In a way, it all started here then?"

He let it fall into the hamper with a flash. At the same moment her cellphone started alarming. It was almost time for closing bell and she hadn't even filled in her grade log yet!

"Oh, crap!"

She started shuffling through her bag, which she had gotten reasonably reorganized during their time together.

"There's Time," said Death languidly.

She silenced the alarm and pulled out her worksheet beginning to fill in the times and responded, "How can you say that? Time is running out!"

"No," said Death. "He is not. In fact, just the opposite. He is here, phasing in near the back of the cavern, just past those moth-ridden piles of unmentionables."

Kristen could indeed see a strange illumination coming from beneath where she lay.

Death lifted the lid of the hamper and leaned way down low to where he could put his unnaturally long arm into the basket. He buried his cloaked arm to the shoulder, and when he came up he had a cardboard sign in his grip.

"Courtesy of our friends over at Lowe and Lomb Inc.," the skeleton said. "They keep the furnaces hot year-round ever since cremation became so popular." He held up a finger, "Excuse me a moment."

Then, she watched as Death disappeared beneath her into the mouth of the cavern before continuing with her forgery.

Near Nan's old pop-up spot, lay an old shoe with the toes missing and a hood ornament in the semblance of Death himself. Directly on top of it a figure in blazing white robes was holding an hourglass and Death could nearly see completely through him.

Death was holding up a cardboard sign that had big black letters that read:

> CHRONOS,
> Check your watch.
> If anyone comes asking...
> You just died. ;)

For a moment Chronos became as solid as Death himself. The incarnation managed to fashion a wink during the split second that their timelines synced up and then passed.

Then, great ellipses of white light began cycling around Chronos' body in spherical waves and the incarnation of Time began fading away as swiftly as he had come.

With that handled, Death turned and dropped the sign beside the huge pile of dusty mismatched socks. He particularly liked a green and red striped tube. He lifted it at arm's length, considered his cold bony feet and dropped it again. It fell beside a rat that was breathing rather laboriously on its back.

As a professional on such matters, he judged it was nearing its end.

"Shame," he said, then he began striding back toward wear he'd left his sickle.

Kristen already had her backpack on and her bicycle by the handlebars when Death returned. Her slicker was stuffed into one strap and her gun was crammed between her shoulders again. According to the time on her cell, she knew she was going to be joining the boys a little late.

Which would be fine, she thought. Maybe they would just start without her and she could go in rogue and attempt to nail John unexpectedly. It wouldn't be the first time anyone had tried.

When she saw the oddly polite Grim Reaper pick up his sickle, she felt a pang of remorse.

"Mr. Death?" she called down to him.

He turned his fleshless face up to her.

"You'd like to know about the raven?" he asked, and then reached back with his left hand and picked up the statuette from the table.

"Well, yes. Er, but I don't think there's time."

"No, there is not. He has gone, continuing on his course to the past. He is the only incarnation that lives backward in time. Which is why I had to make the sign. If I would have simply said what I had to say, he would have actually experienced the words going back into my mouth, rather than the other way around, and as you might imagine, understanding language in reverse is an acquired skill. Unfortunately, Chronos has not been in office for very long. He will get better as he grows younger."

Kristen may have been baffled had she just met the reaper, but this kind of thing hardly phased her now.

"I think you know what I meant."

Death nodded.

"I know what you mean. It's just that parting is such sweet sorrow." He held up the raven. "As far as the story behind this," he turned it in his hand then used the scythe to prop open the lid of the wicker hamper of horrors. "I think you will find that we have come to it quite nicely."

He pitched it in with a flash.

She was not going to cry.

She looked at the time again then stuffed the phone in her slicker pocket. The boys could wait, she just had to know.

"Two things," she said.

Death looked down and his face disappeared under the hood again. There was no yoyo for him to foot anymore, he'd kicked it away earlier on. So, he shuffled his foot a bit then looked back up to her in the semblance that most people see when their real time has come.

However, Kristen's time was still far off.

"The first, I think you know," she told him.

"Your father," said Death.

She would not cry, but didn't dare open her mouth to affirm in fear that the tears would just bleed right out regardless.

"If you had time, I could show you how it works when it is done. But, just know, when I take the soul, it ends the suffering. From there it is weighed and sent up or down unless it is perfectly balanced."

Kristen couldn't believe what she was hearing. At the same time, she could picture her father in those final days. A lot of them were spent in the hospital.

Death continued empathetically, "In the case of balance it goes to purgatory where it is decided by a panel. Those who go south are only there until there debt is paid."

Kristen finally felt that the tears had gone back into hiding under her lids and dared a few simple words, "and Dad? Which, you know, way did he go?"

"You mean, you cannot guess?" asked Death.

And then she thought about it a moment and smiled… and Death nodded.

The reaper thought about telling her that her father's self-sacrificing lifestyle had more than outweighed his other evils, but something told him that she would figure that out on her own. Instead, he asked, "And two?"

"Yeah," she said a bit more hopeful but still confused, "In the story, it seemed like everything was on the up and up. I mean, I know the flood happened before they built our condominium, but I can't help but think that the magic show had something to with all this, and I'm not saying it's all totally bad. But, all of this bullshit." She stretched an arm toward the opening in the banyan's roots and out toward the decimated landscape.

The head under Death's hood shook side to side.

"Happy endings are someone else's beginning to their very own happy ending," he said. Then she remembered her father had promised she'd one day find hers.

Death had paused and Kristen had the urge to pull her writing notebook back out, but he started talking again and she didn't want to miss anything else he might say.

"The world runs forward at an accelerating rate. If you'd been around for the invention of the telegram, for instance, you would have noticed that it didn't take long before there was a world-wide-web, and space exploration. The same thing happened with magic."

Quite fond of her, he thought again.

"Once the word was out, and don't think it wasn't happening everywhere else at once, because it was. That's always been the way of the worlds. Even before different races ever knew of one another's existence, fathers were asking children everywhere to pull their fingers. Likewise, now there are multiple pop-up spots and Rearing Domes, just like this one, all over the globe. In tandem, there exist just as many pop-down spots in Rootworld.

"Anyway, once magic was understood and studied, it became as commonplace as science. In only a handful of years and right about the time that your schoolbooks tell of the flood, it was quickly understood that nesting sites for the young were necessary to better help children cope with and learn respect for both science and magic.

It's a process."

Kristen was starting to get it. She was graduating next year! This was her breakthrough experience!

"The world has many layers. Like an onion," Death continued. "There is a layer out there that is still vibrant with life. When you get your visa and finally cross that bridge, you'll see that the layer most full of life, is always the layer that you are most present in."

Onions? She thought. She doesn't even like onions. What did he say about happy endings? Now she was forgetting. And that's exactly why she always wrote things down!

"People miss you Kristen," he said plainly and that got her attention.

"Your classmates, for example. Your mother. They miss the old you as badly as you miss your father."

She was flabbergasted! Now those damn tears were threatening to bead up again. No, they *had* beaded up again.

Damn him. If he'd have just gotten her with the scythe it would have been less painful!

She would not cry! But this was kind of like dying. Truly believing in magic for the first time was, really, a whole lot like letting go of real life!

"Now," said the Death thing. "You have friends in the woods who are missing you. You should run along, as I have other appointments."

She was trembling, but she nodded. It was terrible, but it was wonderful! And more than anything, it made her think of her father and all of his beloved advice.

She cinched the straps down on her shoulders and started to turn away.

"Oh, and Kristen!" came his voice one final time.

She glanced back into the hole at the pale face with the silver spinning dimes for pupils.

"Do mind the birds."

What Kristen heard was, "Do mind the birds," but what she saw was her Dad. The light behind his face as she sat staring up at him through seven-year-old eyes. Because just then, she had fallen and scraped her knee, but really she was just angry at her little brother.

She saw the face of her father staring down at her and saying, "He doesn't know any better." And Dad drying her tears. Real tears that had begun to flow on Kristen's real cheeks in the real world.

And she saw her dad dry her tears and tickle her until she stopped sulking, and say, "There it is." In her daydream the tears had gone. "You see," Dad said, "things don't have any power over you if you laugh at them."

More real tears broke free from under each of Kristen's eyelids as she pushed her bike out into the light of the real world.

As she started pedaling, more tears followed the damp tracks down her cheeks. The faster her feet went, the faster they flowed.

For once in her life, she didn't feel the need to outrun them.

Down in the shop of Curiosities, Death sighed. Somewhere down by his feet he heard a squeak. Then, a tiny little robed figure scurried its way up the handle of his sickle until it reached his hand and began crawling up toward his shoulder.

Death could now see the little rat's skull under the tiny hood. Then, when the creature perched upright on his shoulder, could feel the tock of the tiny scythe on the tip of his humerus.

He turned his head to acknowledge the Death of rats.

"Didn't make it, did he?"

"Squeak."

"I figured as much," said Death. "Off to your next appointment then?"

"Squeak. Squeak, squeak squeak?"

Death sighed again.

"Yes," he said, "They are not going to be happy. I did this once before and managed to straighten things out eventually, but two? I've never let two go before."

"Squeak!"

"Well," said Death, helping the Death of rats down onto the wooden table. "It's a risky business. Besides, it will only be my second demerit."

"Squeak."

"Oh," he said humbly, "the things we do for love."

From beneath the old Banyan tree came a great flash of light and, just like that, both Deaths were gone.

As Kristen pedaled her way toward the school, a flock of ravens spread out from the old banyan tree over Nan's curiosities and passed over her head in a disorganized chatter far above. She was coming down the slope of ninth street with her face upturned when the squall of feathers reorganized into a dark cloud and settled down into a nearby hollow.

She pulled her bike off onto a gravel drive right at the intersection of ninth and Peters where the birds seemed to have lit. She dismounted and walked her bike down, now following the sound of the chittering and cawing on her left. The gravel drive wound around a bend and back.

She dropped the bike.

There was a dilapidated home in the middle of a bog. By the looks of the place, it had already been discovered by her friends. Hardly a single foot of it had been spared from red, yellow, or blue paint. This must be it! Where Beaver had told her they went to 'bring down the house' after battles.

It was supposed to be a secret, but Kristen had a way of loosening the Beav's lips when she really wanted.

Eew! Not in that way. Between the Beav and Death. Well, she would probably take the latter. Kristen actually chuckled a little bit standing there thinking about it. Maybe she was feeling a little better.

She made her way cautiously down the sloping drive and along the thin margin of shoreline toward the front door. It was extremely slippery, being covered in moss and all. From the front of the house, she could see where the boys would have usually shot up the place. There was a shelf of land on the other side of the bog, just down from where she'd dropped her bicycle. It had a rotted-out wooden railing as if it may have been a balcony before the flooding.

In the trees above, there were ravens. In fact, in the trees behind, there were ravens. Even the trees in front were full of ravens. She supposed whatever she was doing was likely supposed to be being done right here. So, she opened the door of the abandoned home and went inside.

Kristen had been inside of places before, like any ordinary girl might have been, but where she was now could not necessarily be described as inside. Lacking most of the roof and all.

On top of that, Kristen herself no longer felt like some ordinary girl. She had seen Death and at least heard about Time and the Devil. So, when she saw the waif of a woman in the black feather cloak bundled up at the back of the abandoned house, she wasn't the least bit surprised when the being introduced itself as Fate.

FOWL KARMA
Chapter One

War can take place anywhere. A few thousand feet behind an elementary school playground, shots were fired, taking down two young soldiers who had just settled laser sights on the enemy. Only the victims heard the kill-shots. The tearing of camouflage BDUs and the shattering of one's plastic facemask. The attacker was now hundreds of feet away, moving swiftly through the Florida swamp.

John was better than you'd expect. Two tiny red points were playing across the makeshift lean-to where a couple of his snipers lay, their own silenced rifles up on tripods. One had just noticed the dot on his partner when John wedged between them. The stiff sound of a poker card riffle as John squeezed the trigger. Two enemies dropped from a branch-covered blind eighty yards off.

"Shoot *more*," John said, patting Levi's shoulder. Then he was gone again. Always moving.

This last one was going to be a bit more difficult. Wading knee-deep in the bog, John could tell he was in-fact out there, maybe forty yards away or so; after the sound of a gas-powered round, the thin leaves around his head had been shredded. Then came the ripples in the water which told him his target had gone under again. John has a full-face shield with a tiny nipple on the top which can be used as a short-term snorkel. His opponent, one identical.

John went under too, this time all the way. In a single breath he approached an orange band under the murky deep and knew he was on top of him. Surfacing, he recognized the top-facing nipple of his opponent's head. He had come up directly behind him. John pointed his pistol.

The man burst from the deep water as if he were half-fish. John's shot went askew, and with confusion he reached up to steady the clothed and masked mannequin which spun from a short rope under a triggered tree trap.

From under the hanging booby trap, Gunner slickly surfaced, the muzzle of his pistol planted firmly into John's ribs. He squeezed off three rounds point blank. From beneath his body armor, thick red pushed through cloth and mixed with the murk. John doubled over and Gunner caught him, cradling him in the water like a babe.

"Fair and square," John managed to say to Gunner.

John was still looking up at the slowly turning fake-out, which he'd sprung, when Gunner finally said, "Well, look on the bright side. We can still bring down the house."

Then the two had a laugh.

The five boys had been playing paintball with friends all school year. Bringing down the house, was code for shooting up the abandoned home down on 9th St and Peters Ave. The gravel drive was so grown over, you wouldn't know it was back there unless you had stumbled across it while exploring in the woods.

What remained of the architecture was hair on a skeleton. Being unfortunate enough, this single home was fully submerged in the great flood, may have survived had the storm drain not plugged up. The whole property was but two acres of swamp, a bungalow converted to musky mosquito heaven.

Strips of drywall fell into the bog when the paintballs struck. Had the boys had an unlimited supply of ammo, they may literally *bring down* the house. Ammo was always in short supply, but it never prevented them from trying.

Chuck, had a giant mole on his left cheek, and the guys all called him Beaver. He refused to use a firearm, even if it was only powered by CO_2. He always brought a blowgun, like he were some kind of ninja; If only ninjas wore trimmed up trash bags.

Beav was easy to please. He was always happy to just get one round in. If he were lucky enough that the paintball busted, he could happily take ten rounds while retreating.

"Beav, you ain't even gettin' a shot to the wall!" said Levi, eyeing down his sights and squeezing off three of his own.

"That one was totally there!" said Beav.

"It only counts if it bursts, man," Gunner said shooting.

"Yeah, well you try shooting this thing," said Beav, "it takes Stamina."

"I'll tell you what took stamina," said John, "your mom, last night."

"—your mom last night," echoed Beav. Then, with a huge breath, rocketed a stinging shot of yellow paint to Gunner's bare right arm.

Beav had settled for Gunner because no one shot John point blank. John wasn't the biggest, but he was the oldest.

Beav pointed, "Hah! It burst! It burst!"

Gunner aimed his muzzle at the Beav's face and Levi deflected it, "Whoa. whoa. whoa."

"See, I told you it bursts!"

"Yeah, for every one you get to bust, ten roll down the front of our shirts Beav," said Remy. "It's no secret."

"Whatever," Beav said, reloading his blowpipe.

"You might notice if you didn't spend all your time running, Beav," said John.

"Hey, you can't hit what you can't see," said Beav, then he shot one at the house.

A yellow paintball bounced off the side of the Peter's home, and the boys laughed.

Pretty much everyone was sure that Beav only wore those glad bags because he could flip em inside out and pretend he was never hit.

"Guys, look!"

Beav pointed to where a giant raven had lit on one of the standing pillars of the old shed.

John raised his paint pistol, "Five bucks says I nail it."

The boys looked at him in silence as his eye trained down the sight, breathless. The bird watched the boys in the silence.

John finally cracked a smile, letting his finger off of the trigger and opened his eye, exhaling. His gun was coming down when a hiss of CO_2 shot-off behind them and a plume of feathers exploded from the raven's perch.

Remy had pulled the trigger.

In an instant, he had painted the raven's black eye red and it landed, feet sticking up, in the bog. The paint was indistinguishable from blood, if there were any.

"Holy shit!" said Remy, surprised at himself.

No one laughed. They all just stood there, waiting for the bird to move, to struggle.

"Dude, you fucking killed it, Remy," John said.

"You were!"

Beav was dumbstruck, still staring and just shaking his head, "That's bad karma, man."

"Look!" Remy pointed.

The bird had been flinching in the mud.

"That Raven's dead, man," Levi said. "Something's got it!"

They watched as another part of the bog came to life. The tiny green algae began to split along the back and nostrils of an alligator. The water making little black and green arrows in the direction of the bird.

Beav grimaced when the reptile's eyes wiped themselves clean and the gator attempted to get a grip on the raven.

"Quick," said Levi. "Anyone got a tube of pellets?"

"Nah, man," guttered Beav. But they couldn't hear him pleading for them not to do it over the hiss of semi-automatic C02. Remy and Gunner had already started coloring it two shades of red.

John and Beav took a few steps back up the embankment as the gator disappeared. Its attempt at a meal still bobbed in the muck.

"That's bad karma, dudes," said Beav again, following John up the drive. This time they could hear him.

"Guys!" yelled Levi after them. "Wait up."

One by one, the boys followed John up the hill and from inside the Peters home,

the watcher watched.

Chapter Two

"But it's the weekend," John said to his mom over lunch.

"You don't need to go out and get muddy every day of the year, John."

Her look practically dared him not to take his seat at the table. Mac and Cheese wasn't exactly the Doritos and soda he'd score at Remy's. Plus, Remy had a good PC they could keep busy on til Beav got released from captivity at four.

"Sit down, John," Dad said. "A meal with the family won't kill ya for once."

Resigned to wait it out, he tuned out the drawl of parent's obligatory small talk and sat.

John almost had the spoon to his mouth when he saw the black bird with a single red eye, beyond Mom, light outside of the kitchen window.

At that moment, Mom decided to take advantage of John's undivided attention and asked him if he'd considered signing up for the games.

"John?"

She turned to look over her shoulder, but the bird had gone.

Her cell phone was ringing.

"Ug," she said looking at it.

"Well," John said, "Who is it?"

His mother sighed and handed him the phone, then rolled her eyes at his father. "It's Remy."

John took the phone and excused himself.

John's father leaned over the table to his wife and gave her a nudge. "Ya know, I'm starting to think maybe he's a better fit for one of those guilds your sister's been going on about."

Remy was watching YouTube videos of crocodiles preying on antelope when John arrived.

"You called just in time, man," he said. "Mom was just drilling me about signing up for the games again."

"Well, have you?" Remy asked, turning in his desk chair.

"I don't know. Kinda want to hang around for a while," John said, watching a huge croc nab its first victim by the head. "Jesus! Do you think that was a crocodile yesterday?"

"You kiddin?" Remy asked. "This ain't fuckin' Terra Austris!"

"REMY!" came his Mom's voice from the kitchen, "Language!"

"Sorry, Ma!" he called over his shoulder. Turned back and paused it, "It was a gator man." Remy took a swig from a giant mug, "You already have your visa. Plus, you're gonna outmatch anyone in the physical portion. I don't know what you're afraid of."

"Afraid? I'll show you whose afraid, later in the swamp."

John leaned against the desk and tossed a CO2 cartridge up and down. "Nah, I thought, maybe get a job while ya'll are doing senior year, ya know?"

"You know there's no jobs here. What ya gonna do, clean the toilets at the academic center?" Remy said sarcastically.

John tossed the cartridge up again and it seemed to hang in the air for a bit longer than gravity should allow. When it did finally come back down, he fumbled it and it struck the spacebar. The crocodile and antelope thrashed and rolled again on screen.

"Jesus, man. You wanna do another one of my keyboards in?"

"Ah, relax," John tried not to let the video disturb him. "Hey, d'you wanna hear something creepy?"

"You mean, creepier than fluxes in gravity or these crocodiles eating antelope?" Remy asked mashing the spacebar again to pause the raucous. "Strange stuff happens when you don't use your visa, man."

John considered the cartridge for a moment, "You don't think that Paul was telling the truth last year?"

"You've already had your breakthrough!" Remy said, "Keep on denying it, and you'll end up just like him."

True, John had already had his breakthrough experience. It had been in his junior year, when he had been learning to sheer sheep with that druid in Melbourne.

On the second evening, after a meal of cheese curds, the chap had magicked them into the tiny world of lice and fleas by some form of transmogrification. Ever since, John had leaned toward blaming the memory on the mistletoe tea they had ingested prior.

"Well," John said, sliding the cartridge into his pocket. "I don't think my folks would resort to using magic to get me out of the house! But, weird things have been happening." He leaned over Remy's keyboard and punched 'ravens' into the search bar. Then he said, "I think that raven you shot was just outside of my kitchen window."

"Over here, Levi!" Gunner said tugging his sleeve. "Right under there."

"Under where?"

Gunner looked at him like he might have just farted or something.

"Shut up, Gunner!" said Levi, tired of the joke, "and just tell me where you want this thing."

"Well, the way I figure, John'll follow you through here and assume you went down the slope into the water," he pointed with his paint rifle. "But he's gonna stop before he commits to losing the high ground, especially if he sees you out in the bog."

"Okay, so what's your play?"

"We stash that contraption under the roots here and I will hide up the tree in range of the transmitter." He motioned for Levi to give him the bomb. "Then, when he stops to consider his advance, boom."

"My old man must've put a liter of paint in that thing," said Levi. "Ya think it's bad for the swamp?"

"It's a swamp!" said Gunner. "Gotta be a case of empty beer cans down here already."

"Well, ya got me there," Levi said, kicking one out into the water.

"Besides, your old man's last trap was genius! That under-water dummy, finally got him. We'll get him again."

They pushed the contraption under the root.

It really was trash city behind the school. If not for all of the swamp grass, the fact would be even more apparent. Levi couldn't help but notice now, since Gunner mentioned it. A pair of old blue jeans here, a yellowed whiffle ball half buried in the mud. At least the water spiders hadn't vacated.

Their little legs still left needle prick lines through the green algae as they raced away from the two boys' rubber waders. Then there was that creepy mannequin they'd left with absent eyes. Rotating slowly on dingy green line as they walked past.

Something beneath it stirred.

Kristen tightened her brother's facemask to her handlebars. John had shattered hers the night before, leaving a nick under her eye that her mother had been relentless about. Things had smoothed over when she was unusually sweet after dinner. Kristen had spent the evening curled up with her mom on the couch watching an old romance.

She had decided to put in more of an effort after her run-in with Death.

Still, if she were caught hanging out with those boys, it'd be all over. But, she liked the boys. It reminded her of when Dad were alive. Besides, the bag lady she met in the abandon house down on Peters had a pretty good idea how to even up with John. Technically it was a foolproof plan, since Fate pretty much always calls the shots.

Mom thought she'd be heading to Tricia's, but as Fate demands, she never knocked on Tricia's door, and instead, peddled off toward the boys' secret spot.

Beaver had been set free an hour early. TV dinners were his friend.

He looked like a vacuum-packed peanut biking against the wind as he rounded the corner of ninth toward the school. The whipping plastic of his makeshift poncho settled when he stopped on Peters.

He pushed his goggles up on his head. There, alongside the edge of the woods, exactly where she'd purposely left it, was Kristen's bike.

Gunner and Levi watched as a sticky bubble was forming from beneath the spinning mannequin. First undulating in the marsh, and then ballooning to the size of a baseball. Both boys were expecting the thing to pop if it got big enough to strike the underside of the dummy.

From a veiny lime green, the bubble darkened into an inky sac atop the algae. Levi stepped back when he noticed something inside of the bubble move. Gunner had seen it too. Whatever was growing inside of there was looking back at them through slick black eyes. He raised his rifle.

Levi was steadying himself on Gunner's shoulder when something else screamed out from above. It was the red-eyed raven in the trees. Both of the boys saw it up there and stumbled back onto the creek bed.

When Gunner glanced back at the mannequin, he saw a sharp grey beak emerge from the swamp bubble. Backing up the bank, the two boys watched in cold shock as the bog gave some kind of twisted birth to another black crow who croaked a chilling dare, shook the muck from its feathers, and then took flight.

They ran.

Chapter Three

Beav could never have known that Kristen had followed a red-eyed raven down to the old house on Peters avenue. He didn't witness Kristen lean over the shallow swamp and get lost in her own reflection, nor see that reflection change to that of another little girl named Tanner.

Beav wasn't the bravest of the crew, but he had enough guts to skirt the edge of the bog beside the creepy old house in order to be sure the shoe he saw was hers.

In truth, he'd never come this close before. Whatever creepy things were in that mucky water weren't going to stop him now. But getting close enough to pick up the red sneaker, which had been lying on its side by the water, and seeing the two skid marks in the algae was enough for him to go sprinting back up the slope to his bike and race off toward the school.

Levi and Gunner were propped up against the fence by the playground when Beaver let his bike roll to a drop in the weeds.

"Guys," Beaver could tell by the look that Levi was already unsettled. "I think something's happened!"

Gunner simply stood. How could anyone who always dressed like a character from Halo look unsettled, albeit his knee and elbow pads belonged to an old skateboard set?

"Calm down, Haas," said Gunner, a stiff arm out to steady him.

"It's Kristen," Beav said, "I saw her bike down by the Peters home."

When Gunner gave Levi an unsettled look, Beav knew something else was going on as well. He was too tired to even consider what else could be as bad. He slung his bag off to get the shoe.

"What?" he asked the two boys.

Beav looked like he was propositioning Gunner with Cinderella's glass slipper when John and Remy approached behind the school.

"That's not your prince charming," said Remy slapping John on the arm.

"John!" Beav made a beeline for him, clearly unamused with the insult. Gunner didn't seem too entertained either.

"It's Kristen's," said Beav, holding up the red shoe that looked nothing like a glass slipper.

"What are you doing with her shoe?" asked John.

"I found it."

"And you took it?" he asked, "Where was it?"

Remy wasn't feeling quite right about the way Levi was just standing there. It was almost worse than Beav and Gunner not reacting to his joke.

Beav tried again. "She was down by the Peters house."

"Damn it, Beav. I knew you'd end up telling her!"

"No. I found it down by the bog. Next to where Remy creamed that crow."

John reached out and took the sneaker.

That's when Levi finally spoke up. "And that's not all," he said, Gunner giving him a look John had never seen. "Gunner and I, we saw something, too."

Chapter Four

It was strange, Gunner leading the pack down through the woods where they had seen the swamp give birth to a bird.

"I'm telling you, that thing survived the shot, Remy," said Levi. "Gunner and I saw it."

"You guys," whined Beav, "can't we forget about the dumb crows?"

"It's a raven, Beav," said Levi. "Crows don't get that big."

"Who cares? I really think that gator got Kristen," Beav was using a fern as a makeshift rope down the slippery slope. "We should be checking on her."

"We will, Beaver," said Gunner. "It's just right down here."

And there it was…

The geared-up dummy where they'd seen it emerge.

They were standing together at the edge of the muck when John pulled his mask with the snorkel down over his face and started out into the water.

Gunner stiff armed him to a stop.

"Whoa. What are you doing?"

"You said you saw something come from under the trap you got me with. I'm going under to check it out," said John.

"Uh, I don't know if that's such a good idea, man." said Levi.

John eased Gunner's arm down. "C'mon. You said it came up right under there, right?"

Levi's eyes were up in the canopy, now. No sign of the raven.

"Come on, John," Beav said, "there's nothing there. Let's go to the house. That's the real issue here!"

John waded across the marsh. He pushed the foam figure with his index finger. They watched as it bobbed and swung from the sapling, making little ripples each time it scraped the surface.

John *was* going under.

The seconds were like minutes to Levi.

Remy started counting aloud after twenty, "Twenty-two, twenty-three, twenty-four ... "

"Ah, I don't like this, man," said Beav.

The tree dipped as a black bird cut through the sunbeam from above and lit on the sapling. The ripples pushed the algae away from atop of where John was submerged.

Atop the water, a clear image of a young girl rippled out like some mirage in the desert. Remy lost his count and pointed, "Kristen!"

John suddenly broke the surface, dissolving the illusion and sending the bird to wing.

Everyone was screaming. A hail of Gunner and Remy's paintballs were making an arc across the woods after the bird. Adjacent trees were striped with yellow and red.

John yanked his mask off, "What the hell is going on?"

"In the water!" They all chanted in unison, pointing as the image of Kristen spread out into nothingness.

"What?!" John said, turning circles with his hands in the air. He expected to be bit by a moccasin with how everyone was carrying on. Goosebumps crawled up his arms as he trudged to shore.

"Cross my heart, that was Kristen!" belted Beav.

"What? Where?" asked John, dripping.

"On the water ... " Remy said in a reverent whisper. There was a silence that followed. Then he said a bit louder, " ... it *was* Kristen. We all saw it."

The way everyone was standing on the shoreline staring in abject silence, made John feel like the target of a cruel joke.

"You guys aren't making any sense," he said.

"I told you," Beav said. "She's in trouble."

"It should have been the crow," again Remy with the whisper.

"What?" asked John.

"The reflection in the water," he said softly. "It should have been the crow," now with a bit more force, and then certainly, "but it wasn't ... "

"What are you getting at?" asked Gunner.

"John and I read something back at my house," Remy said desperately. "Ravens, crows, and other carrion–"

"I still don't know what's going on!" John said.

Remy put a hand out, "–they're carrion because they carry."

Levi stopped him and tried to clarify.

"Okay, John," he explained, "when you were under, we all saw a mirage in the water. It happened to be when that damn raven landed right on top of you."

"It's what we were shooting at," offered Gunner.

"Ya'll shoulda never shot that Raven, man," said Beav. "I told you it was bad karma!"

"*That* wasn't the raven we shot back at the bog, Beav!" growled Gunner.

"He's right," said Levi. "You can't miss *that* raven. Remy marked it red, permanently."

"Who cares," Beav said. "What about Kristen?"

"I have a bad feeling about Kristen," said Remy. He looked over at John who was still processing.

John finally looked up at them when he felt he fully understood.

"Tell them, John," Remy said.

John turned his head to Remy and sighed.

"What do Ravens carry?"

John thought about his visa. Thought about his friends. Thought about the games. Then he looked up at them.

"Souls ... " he said, " ... souls of the dead."

Chapter Five

As they trudged along the uneven slope toward the Peters home, every black bird Beav saw was the raven.

"There," said Beav, crowding Gunner.

"That bird was tiny," said Levi.

"And it was blue," added Gunner, shrugging him off.

"Well, *I* don't know," he said, stepping into a deep mud hole. "Ah, man!"

Remy was high-stepping it through the brambles, "I told you, man. Weird shit starts happening if you don't fall in line. Ya'll don't believe me, but my Mom does childcare at the Center with Paul's mom and she says—"

"We know what she says, Remy," said Beav, not wanting to hear any more freaky shit. Matter of fact, if he didn't have to hear any more for the rest of the month; that would be nice.

"I'm just saying, Paul swore up and down he wasn't leaving and none of you claim that he ever said goodbye. That's some weird shit if you ask me."

John was doing his best not to think about Kristen. If it was his fault, he wouldn't ever forgive himself.

They were coming upon the old home.

After everything that had happened, the boys saw a different house. The bog was basically a moat, besides one curved pathway to the peninsula where it stood. What once was an old lifeless target, was now a huge face. Two shattered eyes on the second floor, and a ragged gaping grin where they had shot out the front wall. The front door, a solitary tooth.

"That's where I found it," said Beav, pointing. "I had to take the driveway around and inch along the edge there.

As they got closer to the spot, they could make out two black ruts in the mud, skidding away into the water.

"Maybe she slipped?" said Remy, his brow furled.

John surveyed the boys' faces. They were all looking to him for some kind of guidance. He was temporarily out of ideas but he could lighten the mood... Maybe. He pulled back down his snorkel, turning and stepping toward the bog.

"No, no, no ... " all four boys were pleading.

"There's a gator in there, man!'" cried Beav, grabbing John's arm.

John peeled the mask back up over his head and smiled.

"What do you think I'm stupid?" he laughed. "I'm just messin'."

"You asshole," said Gunner shoving him with his gun.

John caught his footing again and took a deep breath then said, "Well," and he placed his hands on his hips craning his neck up. "I guess this means we're winging it."

They all looked up at the moldy siding with John, some crisscrossed at odd angles. With the shape of the place, using the door would feel almost silly, but regardless, John reached out and turned the knob.

    Then… all hell broke loose.

Chapter Six

There were birds. A lot of birds. But no one would see them until after Beav screamed. He was in the back of the pack and still outside after they had been totally covered in birdseed. Someone had emptied a sack full from the upstairs window.

Only John and Levi had avoided it by ducking inside.

"In the water!" Beav had screamed when he saw the reddened Mohawk of reptilian skin emerge from below the surface of the bog and begin carving a path through the algae toward them.

Remy had taken most of the weight of the birdseed, swinging his rifle up at the sound of liquid sandpaper. But, the Beav couldn't take his eyes off of the gator. At least not until the birds exploded out from the front door.

Just inside of the home's empty shell, John and Levi had only a second to make out the shape of a hulking shadow in the back corner of a far room before the cloaked figure raised a hand from amidst its undulating mass of feathers and then exploded into a flurry of living sound. The shudders and slapping of a thousand starving black winged animals moved over the two boys in a torrent toward the sound of food.

Remy slipped in the greasy muck as the wall of birds exploded from inside of the house. Beav shrunk away covering his face. Gunner had completely disappeared from Beav's sight beyond the black feathery torrent that poured through the opening. But even over the countless beating of wings, he could hear the wet slap of his friend Remy landing in the swamp. And this time, Remy's mom wasn't there to yell when he said, "Whoa! Fuck!"

Inside, unscathed, but breathless, John could see that a hunched figure remained in the dark. An old crone in waif's clothing sat perched right along the absent back wall of the home. When she turned and her face caught the twilight coming in from the door, Levi could see that she bore a large red birthmark around her left eye.

Outside, Gunner hadn't waited for the ravens to clear the doorway to start firing. He pelted the swarm of feathers with his semi-auto. The whirling vortex of birds that emerged would have a yellow tint to them if he had anything to do with it!

The paintballs left the chamber by his ear, thwup, thwup, thwup, and he saw the shots explode in the dark mass, but couldn't distinguish which birds he had nailed. The paint simply lifted with the whole conglomeration of birds as they rose.

It was like spray painting a tornado.

Then Remy had splashed down into the bog and Gunner momentarily let off the trigger. His paintballs whipped a rainbow across the water in an attempt to cut off the gator, but the animal sank. Disappearing beneath green whirlpools.

"Shit," he thought.

Beav gave up finding his footing and laid back against the ferns, pulling out the pouch of darts that also fit his blowgun. '*No, I don't like this at all.*' He loaded one in the chamber and aimed through the sea of hopping and pecking karma.

Remy had come up from the bog struggling. He'd lost his rifle and the algae hung from him in ropes that pulled at his face and arms. He felt like he was in one of those nightmares where you're trying to run through syrup or something. Every time he sloughed off a sheet of muck, one tried sucking an article of clothing with it.

You would have thought the gator already had him with how he was thrashing and screaming. Gunner had a foot in the bog and was extending the handle of his own rifle to him.

"Grab hold!"

He reached for the rifle, but it was too late. The nostrils and eyes of the alligator surfaced at once.

Remy froze. He could see himself in the fixed marble mirrors; eyes that remembered him and what he'd done. *'Bad karma,'* was Remy's last thought before the dart from Beav's blowgun buried itself into one of the beast's eyes. The double lid pinched shut in surprise. This time, the red definitely wasn't just paint.

Gunner reached out and snatched Remy's elbow, arm-dragging him from the mud onto the shore.

Kristen had been hiding in the upstairs room of the Peters home, just waiting for her chance to get John. The birdseed had been Fate's idea. But, really when you got down to it, wasn't everything Fate's idea?

She all of a sudden, wasn't so certain.

On the floor by her socked foot, was her creative writing journal. She read off the incarnations to herself:

Death, chilling old dude with humor to die for.

Time, Chronos, was his name, or would be his name if you ever caught up with him, because he lived backwards.

Mother Nature, she's pretty, too. But only in certain seasons.

Kristen was starting to get a feeling in the pit of her stomach.

And then there was Fate. According to Fate, the boys had been coming out and shooting up this home all school year. During their last trip they had started shooting Mother Nature and deserved what was coming to them.

Kristen wasn't so sure she agreed, but Fate had been right about the fact that she would be using her brother's mask today. She had also been right about the shoe scaring Beaver. Fate had been right about the boys being lured here.

Kristen took the first step from upstairs and peered out to where Fate was standing in her billowy feathered cloak. But, something was different about her. Now, there was a big red birthmark over her left eye.

Kristen felt the whole house shift, and thought about how Death had said that Fate was the most attractive of the incarnations. Then she remembered him telling her to keep her wits about her.

She thought she might know exactly what incarnation this was. And for the first time, since her breakthrough, she was scared.

Chapter Seven

Outside, Beav was urging Remy to follow him up the slope and away from the house. The whole structure had visibly taken a deep breath. The strange contraction and expansion sent the ravens up into the surrounding trees.

"They're still in there!" yelled Gunner, his voice drowning under the beat of countless wings again.

Inside, Levi and John watched as the crone's face made room for a giant beak. The tattered garments that she wore grew rigid; her eyes rounded out to smooth eruptions from beneath her lids; one orb ballooned and was glistening red with the boys' fear.

Kristen could see the reflection of their faces in that big red eye as it grew within the crosshairs of her rifle's scope. She was literally seeing red. John and Levi's faces may be plastered all over it, but it wasn't the boys that she was angry at anymore.

It was the Father of lies.

"Be nice," her dad said to her wistful memory. That little thought you get right before squeezing the trigger on an impossible shot. Then Kristen thought of Death laughing at his own joke down there in Nan's old shop of curiosities and she whispered to the air, "This bitch is definitely not your type."

Then she started to laugh.

"C'mon, Remy!"

Beav had retreated from the peninsula and up to their normal ridge.

Remy was caught between his better judgement and his conscious. He had watched Gunner rush into the undulating home after their friends, and now a feathery goliath was raising its wings inside of the crumbling walls. He had to do *something*.

Chapter Eight

The giant, red-eyed raven stabbed at John just as Kristen fired. It tried with a terrible claw to clasp Levi in its grip but Gunner came from nowhere bearing down on it with his semi-automatic. The front entrance crumbled. The main supporting wall buckled against the huge wings which couldn't get a handle on this laughing red haired devil of a girl.

The house was coming down.

The Father of lies shoe-horned gunner with its beak, raising its head and flinging him into the wall. The girl faltered when the boy hit the floor in a lifeless heap. Satan could see the worry on her face. The two other boys had stopped shooting, too.

Game over, thought the incarnation of evil. Then, the four kids felt something raining down on them. Like rice on wedding day.

Remy was throwing great handfuls of birdseed over the wall from the front of the house.

"Come and get it mother fuckers!" he was screaming.

Gunner's body twitched with life and Kristen looked to John and Levi. "Don't let it have power over you guys!" she yelled above the noise and they could see she was forcing a smile.

And the birds came.

Up through the patchwork ceiling, a feathery black whirlwind had formed, like carrion over a certain meal.

The kids were helping Gunner up from the floor when a white and yellow dropping splattered in Kristen's shoulder. The red-eyed raven regained it's footing and was preparing for a great swipe with its left wing, when the splatters started raining heavily down all over.

The raven looked up in surprise. Bird crap was collecting in John's hair. It was covering Gunner's makeshift Halo outift. It was a hailstorm of droppings and they all were now forcing weak smiles when Kristen pointed.

Beyond the Father of Lies was a missing piece of wall, and beyond it, a steep drop into the woods.

"There's our way out of this shit!" said Kristen ducking under the Raven's giant outstretched wing.

The black storm of birds had totally engulfed the house when the four teens jumped.

Beav hopelessly watched as the mass of black birds lit upon every last inch of the wavering Peters home; the structure imploded under the weight. Anything inside had been buried.

Beav took two steps down toward the disaster and then decided against it, grabbing two handfuls of his curly hair.

"Oh, man," he said pacing. "What am I gonna tell Granny?"

About then, Gunner emerged from the woods. His ridiculous but trusty knee and elbow pads scuffed, cracked, and covered in shit. Behind him came John and Levi. Kristen followed.

"Oh, man," Beaver said, dropping his blowgun. "I thought you were goners!"

Blatantly, he ignored John and Gunner's outstretched arms and went straight into Kristen's, who playfully accepted.

"Where the hell is Remy?" John asked. This brought the mood back down to a crawl.

"He was there, and then he was gone," said Beav.

They all watched as the tinted alligator climbed from the swamp and up onto the far shore. It had somehow freed the dart from its eye socket. From behind John, Beav whimpered.

"He wouldn't listen," said Beav. "I told him it was coming down, but he didn't listen!"

The dust from the old cinderblocks was still settling in the new strange silence. Kristen put her face into John's shoulder and Levi stepped up to the old rotten railing.

"Bad karma," whispered Levi, watching the last of the black feathers flutter down amid the brown and grey plumes of wreckage.

"Hey, guys!"

Remy had surfaced from under the bog and was briefly fighting with those ropes of muck again. He tore himself free and trudged up toward the crew with his paint rifle held aloft, "Couldn't leave without this."

Kristen's head jerked up and saw Gunner reach down and offer an arm to Remy, helping hoist him up onto their overlook. This time it was Beav who ran and hugged Remy, oblivious to the filth.

Remy patted Beav on the back gingerly and smiled over his shoulder to everyone else who were just staring. When Beav turned, their stares were loaded with insults, but for once no one said anything.

Then, everyone noticed John staring, and they all turned awestruck at the sight of the destruction of it all.

Then, of course, John said what they all had been thinking.

"Now *that's* how you bring down the house!"

They all laughed.

"Wait, wait …" said Beav, "… that's not all."

He rummaged in his backpack until he finally came up with Kristen's shoe.

"Will you marry us?" he asked, looking up at her.

"Jesus, Beav," said Remy.

"Well, *I* don't know," whined the Beav.

Kristen took her shoe and turned it over in her hands. "You saying I can be on your team, guys?"

"Well, you *are* a good shot," Said Levi.

"I'll settle for just being allowed out of the house the rest of the summer. If Mom finds out I've been with you guys, I will wish I had been eaten by the bird."

They laughed and started the hike back, avoiding the roads, toward the high school.

"Hey," Kristen said, "Why do they call you Beaver anyway?"

"I don't know," said Beav. "I always just thought I kinda looked like a beaver, I guess."

John shoved him playfully from behind, "No, you dumbass. It's because you're like the girl of the group."

"You mean it's a nickname for pussy?!" yelled Beav.

The boys started laughing while Kristen just shook her head full of sweaty hair.

"Well," Beav said, "we actually have ourselves a real girl now so maybe we should…"

"Forget it, Beav," said Gunner. "The name's stayin'"

"Yeah," said Kristen, catching up to walk beside Beav. "I kinda like it."

They strode on a bit until Beav's eyes grew wide and he patted Levi on the shoulder excitedly before saying in John's direction, "Wait a minute! I've got you! I've got you!" then Beav said gaily, "I will bet that's why your parents named you John."

John stopped and turned. Everyone stopped and turned. Kristen and Beaver stopped. John was staring Beaver down coldly.

"What?" Beaver said, his smile fading, "Oh, I didn't mean it, John."

Then everyone started laughing like hell again.

Chapter Nine

The six teens drug their feet through the swamp toward the school until they were close enough to where the whole thing had started.

A dirty pair of blue jeans. The beer cans. The half-buried whiffle ball. The spinning dummy …

But, something was amiss.

All the crews' ammo was depleted. There was always a shortage of ammo.

Then, from up in the bushes, came the crash of leaves. Three guys emerged in full gear with paintball guns raised about twenty yards off. It was the rest of Kristen's old team.

"Traitor!" The squad-lead said behind his mask.

Kristen was too exhausted to even debate.

"Looks like John's crew have finally been caught with their pants down," said the Lead looking left and right to his crew.

John looked at Gunner. The rest of his team shared doleful glances. No one even raised a weapon.

The three men advanced but Gunner lifted his arm and they stopped.

"Game over for today boys," he said as Levi eyed the bomb they had stashed under the root earlier that day.

Then he pressed the detonator, and the swamp water ran red with instant victory.

"You sure that's not bad for the swamp?" asked Levi.

"Who cares," said Gunner. "I'm ready for bed. Besides, it's a swamp!"

Thanksgiving break came quick during the next school year. John had decided to join the Hunter's guild, much to his father's delight, so he was off in some other universe, apparently. One where magic came long before science, so things made better sense.

Since that was the case, he wasn't present when the crew gathered at Remy's for the big meal.

Kristen however was arguing with Beav over who gets first dibbs on the deviled eggs while Remy's mom was bringing out the grub.

"So, Kristen," said Gunner, scooping some mashed potatoes, "you think about what you're gonna do after graduation?"

Kristen had opened her mouth but Beav cut her off, "Do ya think you could take off the elbow pads at the dinner table, at least?"

Gunner flopped the steamy spoonful onto his plate and hiked the spoon back into the bowl. Then he pushed up his elbow pads a little and gave Beav the up yours sign.

"Well," Kristen said, as Levi was motioning to pass the rolls, but he too cut her off.

"What was it John said about our world coming after theirs?" he asked in general.

Kristen grabbed a deviled egg while Beav was preoccupied with philosophy. Beav said, "He says the Druids had to create our world to give the Romans somewhere to grow up."

Beav gave Kristen a look then grabbed his own egg before passing the tray to Remy. "Yeah but, Rootworld? Not a very original name."

Remy smashed a whole egg in his mouth.

"Like a tree," said Levi grabbing the tray, "that world is the roots." Then he started passing it along. "Besides, I don't think they really conjured up Earth. It's gotta be like the chicken and the egg thing."

The tray went to Gunner who said, "Yeah. That makes sense. But, what about gravity? If they don't believe in gravity, then what holds things together over there?"

Remy's mom came into the room. "I've heard that the Arch Druid and the King hold things together over there for the most part," she said, placing the turkey on the table. "But I believe it is actually Mott. She can be pretty threatening with a frying pan."

They all looked like someone might have farted.

Then Gunner said, "So, Kristen?"

She had been waiting for her turn to speak, and she had the perfect answer for a perfectly sensible girl.

"I was kinda thinking I would hang around for awhile," she said.

"You gotta be shittin' me!" said Remy.

"REMY!" yelled his mom, "language!"

"Sorry ma."

And they all had a laugh.

THE END

Epilogue

Outside of the barriers, the world had changed.

Most of the World's magicians and philosophers describe the current shape of the planet as a giant "C". Which is ironic because most of the scientists, geologists, and other professors ending in "ists" agree. Only they would spell it longhand.

The fact was, the World *is* mostly covered by the sea, but it always had been, hadn't it? The only difference now was that all the land had been twisted back up together into Pangea when the great pyramid rose from the desert. It now stood so high that it touched the heavens, well, metaphorically speaking.

Who could know that all that dribble about the tower of Babel being cast down by the hand of God, were true?

Who could know that the God who'd done it might have been an apprentice druid from the Rootworld who was mucking around at a time that he should have been studying his Ogham Alphabet?

Either way, the rising of the Great Pyramid was a friendly signal to the inhabitants of the Rootworld, as the Druid's entire universe had been calculated to resemble just such a structure.

In fact, the eldest Priests of the Sun were so certain of it that they had, at one time, built a pyramid among the branches of an ancient Beech tree in hopes that its reaching toward their own sun would eventually deliver them to their own great Originator, just so long as they didn't over water it, that was. They too, would eventually be disappointed. As you can imagine, anyone who has ever been born has no business trying to climb back into whatever orifice they emerged from. I mean, that would only be common sense!

So, imagine their reaction when the Great pyramid of Giza ended up being only the tip of an unfathomable ancient endeavor, and it twisted up from the desert like a screw, drawing all of the continents together again in a giant dance.

A great pyramid at the center of a round world!

Well, that must mean that someone up there believes in magic! While on the Globe, science was dying, in the Rootworld, science was only just being born.

Author's Notes

First off, writing this compilation of short stories occurred over the span of a few years. Only after I had started submitting Tanner and the Hamper of Horrors as a standalone novella and began getting rejections from literary agents, did I start considering combining it with other books I had previously self-published in the horror genre.

It had been difficult getting any bites on works under 50,000 words, and most of my writing ends right around 30,000. I think it is because of the scant way I use my adverbs and adjectives.

Over the last ten years or so, I started using more narrative to allow actions and definitions to present themselves. Honestly, I think it was after I tried reading War and Peace and gave up about a third of the way through. I have probably gone from reading one or two fiction books a month to reading that number of books every week. Plus, articles, poetry and hair spray bottles when I forget the newspaper on the way to the shitter.

Also, I think the adversity in my life has attributed to most of my creativity. I think about the inspirational reading I did that contributed to this piece and wonder just how much shit Stephen King, Terry Pratchett, and Piers Anthony were putting up with in their own day to day's. Their wives and families more than likely deserve a mention as well.

I am sure that there will be many people, especially fans of Anthony's and the late Sir Pratchett's, that are wondering if I plan on writing more in worlds so similar. The answer is, yes.

Any reader will notice that the core narrative in this book is leaning toward satire, while the short stories have a Stephen King or Anne Rice type of narrative feel. It has to do with the evolution of my reading and writing.

In fact, I wrote Twits Do It Better in a style that any reader of Pratchett's will appreciate and recognize. It was written more recently. The reader will soon see that Arthur: A Rootworld Novel, will be the first novel in my opposing magical land that is written in my totally evolved style of satire and comparative to the Discworld, complete with footnotes. So, there's that.

However, I do feel that I may venture into this strange and magical world of pop-up spots. Sir Terry did something amazing when he started his Discworld series and created round world from there. What I have done is start from the real world, in a sense. Will I dare to go into his old place? I don't think it's possible to do.

No one has done it because he's so hard to hold a torch to. But I think I can use my new Death character, which is a blend of both Pratchett's and Anthony's version to help us reminisce some more in my future tales. Especially, if we manage to weave our way between a flat earth (the Rootworld) and a round earth (the Globe) once again.

Thank you, Reader! You deserve the biggest commendation. I am a true believer that reading makes you empathetic. Once, during an interview for a fire-fighting position, the only question that mattered if you got right was:

What is the one thing that will never change about public service? The golden answer was Empathy. Because without it, computers or trained monkeys could do our jobs just as well.

Read and learn to love others. We deserve it.

See ya on the next adventure!   -Jay Horne